THE ARRIVAL

Collection of Short Stories

A N PRASANNA

TRANSLATED BY
JANHAVI LAKSHMINARAYANAN

CLEVER FOX PUBLISHING
Chennai, India

Published by CLEVER FOX PUBLISHING 2024
Copyright © A N Prasanna 2024

All Rights Reserved.
ISBN: 978-93-56485-91-4

This book has been published with all reasonable efforts taken to make the material error-free after the consent of the author. No part of this book shall be used, reproduced in any manner whatsoever without written permission from the author, except in the case of brief quotations embodied in critical articles and reviews.

The Author of this book is solely responsible and liable for its content including but not limited to the views, representations, descriptions, statements, information, opinions and references ["Content"]. The Content of this book shall not constitute or be construed or deemed to reflect the opinion or expression of the Publisher or Editor. Neither the Publisher nor Editor endorse or approve the Content of this book or guarantee the reliability, accuracy or completeness of the Content published herein and do not make any representations or warranties of any kind, express or implied, including but not limited to the implied warranties of merchantability, fitness for a particular purpose. The Publisher and Editor shall not be liable whatsoever for any errors, omissions, whether such errors or omissions result from negligence, accident, or any other cause or claims for loss or damages of any kind, including without limitation, indirect or consequential loss or damage arising out of use, inability to use, or about the reliability, accuracy or sufficiency of the information contained in this book.

ABOUT THE AUTHOR

A. N. Prasanna

$\mathcal{A}$.N. Prasanna was born in 1943. A graduate in Electrical Engineering, he is interested in literature, theatre and cinema. He has published seven collections of short stories. He has been conferred many significant awards. He translated Gabriel Garcia Marquez`s Nobel Prize Winning Novel *One Hundred Years of Solitude* into Kannada. He wrote the script and directed a TV Series and a feature film. He has written critical articles on award-winning films in international film festivals of the previous and the present century. He served as a member of the jury of the Asian Films Awards at the 6th International Film Festival, Bengaluru.

ACKNOWLEDGEMENT

I wholeheartedly thank Ms. Janhavi Lakshminarayanan for all the efforts in translating the stories.

I express my thanks to M. R. Rakshith who helped a lot during the entire process of completion of the formalities for publication.

I extend my thanks to Sri H. V. Lakshminarayana (Alaka Thirthahalli) and Sri M. S. Raju for their reaction to the stories and the support they expressed for publication.

I thank Clever Fox Publishing Pvt. Ltd., and their various personnel for their effort towards publication.

A. N. Prasanna
E-Mail : prasanna450@gmail.com
Mob : +91 9880504463

CONTENTS

The Search 1

The Freedom 27

The Park 46

The Turn 65

The Arrival 82

The Monsoon 106

Rathasapthami 138

A Visit To The River 154

A Little This Way And That 165

The Shift 196

The Search

*L*ately, Sukrutha felt like she was cheating herself if she didn't make a decision, and that feeling left her without any scope for distraction. In a split second, the glow of that decision was born. It opened its eyes, grew faster than anyone could imagine, and made its home in her mind. For a second, it made her disoriented and made her head spin round and round, noisily, spreading an unknown fear, excitement and rhythm of a strange tune running through her body. Since she had created this strange situation herself, she felt it would be wonderful if it reached its final goal. She also felt that she had her own individuality, and that's probably why she could never accept anything without a reason. It wasn't clear what set her apart, although she looked like anyone else and nothing special. The policy of 'Make hay while the sun shines' without heeding to her wishes and letting her secrets lie beneath the ground she was trying to stand on was long uprooted from her system.

She was certain no matter what others felt, she had to face the most important challenge of her life. She felt that the wins and losses due to this would significantly shape her personality-- either reach great heights or hang her head in shame for the rest of her life. She had to face this single-handedly instead of living in denial, as though she was wearing a mask in front of the world.

Also, this thought was not short-lived. She had to take the high road to get out of the mindset surrounding her. If she leaned towards taking the crossroad to somehow reach a solution to her problem, not only would she be a fool, but she should be prepared to make a fool out of everybody very close to her as well. To add to it, she would have to spend her entire life putting up a front. Even that could only be done if she lived quietly and adjusted to everything. Even if she did that, how could she face herself? How could she escape her own face that appeared in her mind even if she closed her eyes? She definitely didn't want that and took the opposite stance. She was aware that she took this decision in line with her overall life. Sometimes, this agitated her. Her decision was not something that could be announced. It was her personal stance. Also, there was no way of moving away from it. Despite the fact that it was related to her future, she felt that it also involved another soul. She was sure that it would impact that person's mind and overall personality as well. She would explain it to herself in this very simple way: the stream of life is silvery white. What happens if a light passes through colored glass? The color of the light changes, right? How did the colored glass come in the way of this light? Whatever the reason, it did. Now, how to proceed under such circumstances? Everything becomes beautiful only if it unites with another coloured light. She often made it clear to herself that if a colored light desires a silver light instead, it becomes a sham.

Just then, Nayana got up from bed, washed her face and headed to the kitchen as usual to check on the coffee preparation; she took over and turned the flame to low in order to keep the coffee hot. She saw Sukrutha quietly sitting and gazing out of the window and went in and got another cup of coffee. When Sukrutha continued to ignore her, even when Nayana brought her cup of coffee and held it in front of her, she said a bit loudly, "What *ammanni*? Looks like you are on a world tour. Here, take it…" She placed the cup on the table. She observed that Sukrutha got up hastily, looking at the wall clock and went on to say, "If you continue to sit like this, the Sun will rise above our heads, and nobody will be around to shake you awake. Get up."

Sukrutha wondered if the environment of the house also contributed towards her decision. Her mother, Rajamma, always tried to bring any issue onto the streets. She would seek all support in order to achieve it. She ensured that the guests who visited her house would sit facing a particular direction only; she was such an ardent follower of Vaastu Shastra. Her entire work and conversations were based solely on this premise. Krishna Kumar, her father, was the exact opposite. Everything had to be in order and especially pleasing to one's mind. He was particular that nobody and no force should come in the way. Sukrutha felt that this was totally unrelated to him being an architect.

Rajamma did not want her family to be special in any way. She was content if they were like most others. She used to tell Sukrutha at least a few times a day, "Look, this year, you must get married." To which she would reply, "Done? Have you finished with today's quota?" Rajamma was not particular about who the *beegaru* (daughter's in-laws) would be or that the *vara* (bridegroom) had to be a certain way. Her mindset was modern enough to allow Sukrutha to choose her own. Especially father Krishna Kumar said, "It's entirely your wish… as your mind says," and gave her complete freedom. Apart from that, her older brother

Vishwanath, who had no plans of getting married for a few more years and Nayana, who was studying in college, had no opinion. Overall, the responsibility of selecting her partner was solely on her. She had decided to make full use of the situation.

These thoughts swirled around in her head as Sukrutha cleaned the room (which she shared with Nayana) mechanically and walked out of the room. As she heard the noise of the mixer that her mother was using, she saw some clothes piled in front of the washing machine. She loaded the clothes into the machine and asked, "Is that all? Can I switch it on?" Rajamma nodded. She switched on the washing machine, ate the breakfast that her mother had kept on the dining table and took her moped out to the street; this completed one chapter in the morning.

Not only was she used to looking ahead on the road, but she also kept an eye on the vehicles that moved on either side. She encountered chaos all the way to the office. She felt a sense of relief as she parked the moped in the orderly parking lot.

She felt like she was on another planet even as she entered the lift after climbing a few steps. She wasn't relaxed enough to notice who was in the lift with her. Even when she reached her floor, she was reminded by someone else. "Thanks…" she said and stepped into her office. For some reason, the office, which was a part of her daily life, seemed to have taken on a different shade.

The office environment, where even the drop of a pin could usually be heard, was enveloped by a murmur. The office consisted of around fifty cubicles separated by cardboard panels. The laptop was her constant companion there. Sukrutha found it strange that the situation of sitting with the laptop, focusing on work against the ever-ticking time while trying to meet the deadlines, had changed so suddenly. Even before she could ask, "Wish in advance. Sampath is getting married," said Bhavya, who got married the previous year. The air around touched the smile on Sampath's face as he was getting ready to enter a whole new world. For a split second, Sukrutha was overcome with a plethora of feelings. Of late, especially since morning, she was immersed in the myriad coloured weaving in her mind, and it took her a few seconds to come to reality. When Sampath gave her the wedding card, she smiled lightly and said, "Hearty congrats."

As she began to get back to work, Bhavya came up to her and said, "It's your turn next." She raised her eyebrows as she said, "I know your entire family; there's no problem. Why are you waiting?" "No, no, next is my turn," said Sukrutha, meeting Bhavya's smile with hers. "That is the spirit," said Bhavya as she put her hand on her shoulder, leaned in and said, "Look, I know some information regarding Sampath's wedding… it seems he does not want to marry her, and she does not want to marry him. When asked why, both of them claim that they know something undesirable about the other. Who can say what is true and what is not in this?" she whispered and walked away.

Sukrutha stopped dilly-dallying and postponing and took up what she had to do for a long time. As she began, everyone else in the office seemed to disappear, and she was all alone. The laptop felt like a big blackboard. On that board, along with her photograph, she wrote all her details with a piece of chalk. As she wrote all this, she giggled with a strange sense of excitement. She sat quietly for a few minutes. Finally, when she wrote 'Conditions apply' in a larger font, she was exhausted. She felt like closing her eyes. Just because she wanted shelter, she did not have the heart to take the support of a lie and pretend. She felt like she was flying high above to reach an unknown city. The vague figure at a distance was perfect. It just had to come to life. It was so special that nobody else could breathe life into it and had to do it by itself. It took immense courage to walk on such a path where there was no path. It was preparing itself for a different mould. Only if such a thing was given did the figure get different kinds of strengths. It brought a flash to the eyes, soothing heat to spoken words, several avenues to walk, the smiling flowers on all the surrounding plants, trees and branches, and the gentle whispers that go along with their intoxicating perfumes.

Sukrutha was brought back to reality only when Bhavya approached her and said, "Come on. Hope you have brought your lunch box." Only then did her ears perk up to hear the sounds of her own footsteps, along with all the other sounds.

Long back, I was in another world. I was then pushed into a different world. Now I am trying to create a world of my own, she thought. Suddenly, she felt happy that her efforts had borne fruit. When she happened to see Sampath, she gave a wide smile and said, "You must give a separate party for the office colleagues. Hope you know." Later, when she met Bhavya, she said, "As per your advice, I have entered the field." Although Bhavya was surprised, since she had a hunch about it, she said, "Very good. All the best!"

The shops seen outside seemed to paint the outer walls of the office with a new colour, the flying birds seemed to have gained a new force and vitality in their wings, the youngsters' dresses seemed to have a new impression, the occasional sounds of vehicles seemed to have mingled with a happy tune, the eyebrows of the girls who passed by seemed to have spread a festive excitement.

When she went home and broke the same news, Rajamma was thrilled and said, "*Maharayathi* (Madam)… finally, you made up your mind." Krishna Kumar smiled a little more than usual and said, "Hope for the best." Nayana said, "Which site have you registered? I want to see," she insisted. Since it was different from the usual, she wondered if it was right to tell her, and then decided that it was anyway up to her to explain it however she wanted and gave her the details. Within a few minutes, Nayana approached her again and said, "Hey, what is this? It says conditions apply. What does it mean?" Sukrutha forcefully laughed and said, "You always say that I'm special. That's why I'm looking for someone special." Nayana was baffled. She said, "I don't understand this…" and then she told everyone else at home about it. When they asked her, Sukrutha said, "This is about my marriage, right? It is totally private…" and stopped.

It didn't take long for people in the office to hear about 'Conditions apply' from Bhavya. It wasn't as easy to handle it in the office. Those who held a favourable opinion about her were broadminded about it, and those who thought otherwise took the opportunity to talk bitterly about her and said, "She is so arrogant as if she will find someone that nobody else can." But Sukrutha did not take any of this seriously. Even when she wrote it, she had an idea about how people would react in her office. But when it actually happened, she was a bit upset. Such reactions in the office faded very quickly because everyone had their own problems. Or some other exciting news must have grabbed their attention. Sukrutha was just relieved that she got out.

The lights that hung down the walls of the office, the wide and tall pictures, the rotating chairs, and the notebooks on the table tops discussed among themselves the unpleasantness that Sukrutha had faced from others. Overall, with rapt attention, they showed support and cooperation for Sukrutha's initiative. When she looked at them, they just gave her a bright smile.

During this time, did anyone respond to the post on the matrimonial site? And if they did, she was curious and eager to see how it would be. Not only did she look forward to seeing what kind of response she would get, but she knew that the person would definitely expect a reaction from her, too. As soon as she began to think of how she could open up, many thoughts enveloped her. Her thoughts came to an abrupt halt as she came face-to-face with that day's situation. She did not realise then that her entire personality would change as a result of that, and she would have to think of how to behave in front of others. When it was destroyed to that extent, she felt that there was no way to solve it.

She was totally convinced that she had no other way than to be honest. She couldn't think of any other way to protect her personality other than the one that she had taken. How can she protect her individuality while facing such a situation? For that, even if the talk and situation went to the extreme, she decided not to give up on her decision and her stance. More than anything else, she loved the decision that she had taken. She felt proud that despite all the confusion and disturbances from the incident, the shame she might have to face in society, the possibility of having a hopeless future and so on, she had taken this first step. She felt that whenever anyone expected a response from her, she should make herself strong enough to tell him about her "condition" without any hesitation or fear. It wasn't as easy as she thought or said, but she felt there was no other way.

When she chose this path, was it possible for her to explain the past story, its relevance and her position to anyone? Could she tell her mother? Or could she share it with her father, sister or brother? This situation will never go away. At such a time, nothing could be said if asked why she did not share it with anyone else. A decision to put all this aside and continue to shape her life and future wasn't the answer.

Just as she accepted her family for what they were, it's only fair that they accepted her just the way she was. If such was not the case, what could be said for those meaningless words and relationships? If the family relationships were of a kind, the relationship she was seeking was much deeper and more personal, much more special than the relationship with her family.

With these thoughts swirling in her mind, she opened her laptop to check if there were any responses. Some of them had directly asked, 'What is your condition? You can write or call and let me know.' If she wanted to tell them, wouldn't she have mentioned it already? She didn't know how to react to such meaningless questions. In the midst of all these, a few had responded, 'Whatever your conditions may be, I would like to hear it in person. Let's meet. Let me know the place and time.' No matter what such a person looked like, she felt it best to meet him in person based on her previous experience. She wondered if he wanted to meet just any girl and talk. Immediately, she thought that it was not right to unnecessarily doubt the person. She replied, 'Let's meet,' and for the first person among them, she replied, 'Would this weekend, Saturday morning at eleven, be convenient for you?' She got a confirmation faster than she had expected. That made her eyebrows twitch a little!

As she had fixed up earlier, she had to meet Vikram in Coffee Day at half past six that evening. Right from the afternoon, she began preparing herself mentally. No matter how much she weighed on it, her thoughts kept revolving around one central point. As she couldn't concentrate on her office work, she kept making many mistakes. She was tired of correcting the same mistakes over and over again. She sat quietly. Bhavya, who came to discuss some office matters, said, "Looks like you are deep in your thoughts… you can tell me about it if you want." Sukrutha immediately gathered herself together and said, "It's just nothing…" Yet, Bhavya stared at her and went back to her desk.

When Sukrutha looked up, she felt that the still air was getting hotter. She felt as if the filing shelf that was kept at a little distance and all other office items that were placed on top of it were talking about her in hushed tones. They, too, seemed to look curiously at Sukrutha, who was in another world. She forced a laugh as if to convince them.

Then she looked at her watch to check if it was time to leave the office. As she looked out of the window, she saw a few faded flowers, withered leaves that had fallen from the tree, and some drooping trees at a distance, as if it was very difficult for them to raise their heads. Somehow, it seemed like the wait was going to be a long one.

Later, as she entered Coffee Day, she looked around to check whether Vikram had already come. He hadn't yet come. She hadn't prepared herself in any way for this meeting. She didn't see the need to do that either. Just as she was wondering whether he would actually come, the oval-faced, thick-haired, five and a-half feet tall and regular build Vikram entered. Even from that distance, they recognised and waved at each other. Then Vikram sat opposite to her. Not knowing what to say, they sat in silence for a few seconds. Then Vikram said, "It's very nice to meet you." Although she didn't think these words of polite conversation were special, she said, "Likewise." Then, for a while, they spoke about their jobs.

They ordered coffee when the waiter approached their table. Both of them took time to come to the main point of conversation. Finally, Sukrutha said, "I've told you everything else. I'd like to reiterate that conditions apply," and became silent for a moment.

Already, a series of images compelled her to impose the conditions paraded in her mind. Her mind was filled with thoughts of her friend Radhika's husband, who had behaved in the most unexpected way without giving her an inkling of doubt earlier. Even to that day, the doubt whether her behaviour had, in any way, given him a signal to bring about the sudden attack nagged her. Radhika was her friend, and she trusted them and asked her husband and Sukrutha to go to her house. She wondered that although she did not have any immoral thoughts, what about him? She didn't think he had such thoughts earlier, either. That day's incident left her eyes, mind and thoughts helpless. Her body had crumbled, simply defeated. She had lost her sense of self. She only remembered the deafening noises forcefully entering her ears, and she had fainted. Now, it was just history. But it was not something that she could share with anyone. She couldn't fathom what was on his mind as he destroyed everything. Even her friend, who joined them later, was perplexed. If she felt defeated, her friend seemed to be equally defeated. Even as the moments that had just passed seemed to take over her again, Radhika tried to console her with a lot of compassion, and she shouted at her husband with equal harshness and drove him out of the house. The words were so full of terror; she had decided never to meet him again in her entire life. Although this issue concerned Radhika and her husband, there seemed to be no way to correct her own fate and the loss that she herself had faced.

It took every ounce of her energy to continue the conversation with Vikram, who sat in front of her, as she remembered that fateful day. She gulped, looked at Vikram, bent her head slightly and said, "I had mentioned that conditions apply." He said, "That's what I asked. What are the conditions?" She wondered how it would be to continue the conversation by posing a question. She gathered her courage and asked, "It's just mainly about the physical relationship between a man and a woman. What is your opinion about that?" Vikram was not prepared for that question. The question confused him. He was speechless. For a few seconds, neither of them said anything as if stuck in a wordless spot. Even the air stopped moving around them. Curious to know what the next words would be, the air seemed to stand still, with its ears perked up.

Both of them looked away, avoiding each other's eyes. Then Vikram said, "If you tell me what is **on** your mind, I'll tell you mine."

Sukrutha replied, "The very first stage of my condition is that…"

"I didn't understand."

"Oh no. It is quite clear. Only if you have a clear idea and experience can we proceed further."

By the time she finished talking, he was stunned and turned his face away. She observed this and felt it was meaningless to continue. She felt as if all kinds of hopes, preparation and so on had been razed to the ground that day.

"Before you know my condition, are you ready to talk openly with me and be honest about your situation? Decide and let me know."

"For that, can we meet again?"

"If you want…" said Sukrutha.

Vikram stood up quietly and left after wishing her. Sukrutha continued to sit, trying to recover. At that time, none of the noises or sounds in Coffee Day touched her mind. A few minutes rolled by, and then she got up and left.

When she stepped out, suddenly, many different noises filled her ears. She felt as if each and every figure appeared much larger and came rushing towards her. Unable to bear the sights and sounds, she closed her eyes for a few seconds.

She wondered how she could shape her future when the very first person she met was like this. Just as she was a unique person, even others were unique. They have had their own experiences, feelings, viewpoints, future ideas, standing in society, prestige and so on, that are important to them. Only those who take these things lightly and have the strength to give utmost importance to a life of honesty were the only ones who would appeal to her. But that was not the only factor that decided everything. That honest person must also be experienced, as she wished. Such a person must come forward. Otherwise, a kind of defeat, hesitation, and sense of inferiority would never leave her.

Sukrutha did not believe in taking a step back from what she had undertaken just because of the first setback. She became firm regarding her decision. She repeated to herself that, more than anything else, she would not live without being honestly in love.

Sukrutha's moped took the way back home as a force of habit. As she entered, her entire family gave her a burning look. Nayana said, "Oh, you came? We thought that you had forgotten the way back home." She looked at her watch. She had never gone away for so long without informing anyone at home. So she said, "Sorry, I had some work… didn't even realise the time…" to which Nayana replied, "In another half an hour, I would have lodged a police complaint." Rajamma gestured for her to stay quiet and said, "Come, have something to eat and sleep. No more talk." And that silenced everybody.

As the day began, and she was in a rush, the mobile rang. Just when she didn't want to talk to anyone, she wondered who called and looked at it. "*Arre*! Radhika…" She picked up to answer the phone, feeling happy and excited. "I know you weren't expecting my call, but how can I keep quiet after all this has happened? That's why I called," said Radhika from the other side.

"Okay. Tell me what is the matter, in just one second. Give me the details later."

"Can't tell over the phone… everything face-to-face… *khullam khulla* (openly). Be ready. I'll see you soon," she said and cut the call.

She wondered why she called now after so many days if she only had this much to say. It was a kind of suffering then. Now, it's a different kind of suffering, she thought.

What does she get by tormenting me this way? Some strange friendship doesn't let go even if I want to escape. Who knows what is bothering her? Whatever it is, she should have hinted subtly or in just one word at least, she thought angrily.

That day, she had a meeting in her office. While getting ready, she couldn't keep the unwanted thoughts of Radhika's mysterious behaviour, the possible reason and the previous day's fruitless meeting with Vikram out of her mind. Trying her level best to suppress her thoughts, she continued to get ready for the office work.

During the meeting, which started on time, she found it difficult to control her wandering mind. After the meeting, as everyone got up to leave, her boss sent the office boy to call her. He said, "Looks like you are very worried about something." To which she replied, "No, sir." He went on, "I could figure it out by the way you were at the meeting. Whatever it is, don't take it to heart," and ended the conversation. She felt ashamed that she was behaving in such a way in public that it was obvious to everyone. Somehow, she surrendered to silence during most of her working hours and then left for home. Even there, she didn't talk much to anyone due to the experience of the day. Before going to bed at night, she opened her laptop and found a meeting invite from someone called Jagannath. Although she felt a bit curious, she wasn't as tensed as she felt the first time. Yet she felt it was her responsibility to reply, and she sent him an email asking him to meet her the following evening at seven, at Kamath Hotel opposite the main circle. Even then, the next day at work, she didn't feel a rush. She felt that whatever it was, she'd deal with it in the evening.

By the time she reached the assigned spot in the evening, she saw that the round-faced, small-eyed, medium-built Jagannath had already reached. As she knew that waiting was unwanted and exasperating, she felt a little bad for being late. She walked up as usual with a fixed smile on her face and wished him. But she found lines of greater excitement on Jagannath's face. They looked around and found a corner to sit. Jagannath started the conversation. For a few minutes, they exchanged information about their work. Then Jagannath said, "The profile description that you have given is very interesting." To which she said, "Looks like it."

A few seconds passed. Then Jagannath said, "What are your conditions… can you please tell?"

"The conditions are… very simple. I have some opinions about the relationship between a man and a woman. Especially with respect to the one I'm getting married to, I have my own stand."

"I don't understand. Can you please explain what you mean by that?"

"First of all, we must open up our hearts in order to understand each other, especially about very personal matters…"

"Excuse me… I still didn't understand…"

"I'll make it clear. I have my own stand when it comes to physical relationships between a man and a woman."

He stared at her.

"If I have to tell you about my conditions on this, it's about whether the life partner that I'm looking for has already had such an experience even before marriage. It is very important to me."

"Meaning…?"

"Assuming that, in the first stage, the man and woman are both interested in getting married. If they've already had such an experience, then it is not right to keep it a secret. There will be meaning in their relationship only if they are open with each other."

He sat without saying much.

"What if the girl you would like to marry has already had such an experience?" she asked and looked at him keenly.

He sat with his neck bent as if he just couldn't believe what he heard and was trying to grasp the meaning. Then it all flashed to him, and he said, "So, you mean to say…"

"There is no need to explain this. I've already told you. We just have to apply what was said generally to each other."

As her words sunk in, he stopped the conversation, unable to continue. He said, "All the best…" and looked away.

Later, they just silently gulped down the coffee that the waiter had already served.

Jagannath said, "I'll think it over and let you know," and left. As he got up and walked away, Sukrutha could guess, by his gait, what his decision would be. She smiled weirdly as she got up and painfully stepped towards the small, lit-up coloured bulbs.

Jagannath was shocked by the meeting he just had. He didn't have any inkling that he might come across such a situation. The words that he had never before heard or seen left him dumbstruck. He asked himself if anyone could live like this; for this, does he have to silence his thoughts and answer, is it possible for him to open up all that is within? This seems to be a very difficult issue, he thought and left. For the next two days, Sukrutha did not get any email or phone calls from anyone to meet in this regard.

That day, being a weekend morning, the mood in Sukrutha's house was relaxed. Just then, her mobile rang, and she picked it up to see that it was Radhika! All of a sudden, many intense waves of emotions rose up in Sukrutha's mind. She picked up the phone with the thought of how she troubled her every time she called by not giving out any details. On the other side, Radhika said, "Look, I've been telling you that I'll visit. I'll come to your house this evening; no, *we* will come." Sukrutha felt that her words sounded cryptic, just like before. Then she immediately remembered that Radhika had a five-year-old son and thought that might be the reason she said so. She forcibly laughed and said, "I will be waiting for you all. Don't miss…" and told everyone at home about Radhika's visit. As she looked around, it seemed like there was a blend of perfumes in the air. Her longtime friend is coming now. Since they last met, she must have had so many special occasions. If nothing else, she has her dearest son with her at all times. What more does she need? She wondered. But then another thought followed. Just because of the incident that happened back then, did she make the right decision to keep him away? She had stood by Sukrutha as a pillar despite her own pain and anguish. She had also decided never to see her husband ever again, even if it meant that she would be single for the rest of her life. She had understood Sukrutha's feelings and her loss. Nobody else in the house knew these details, and they remained between them. Her family only knew Radhika as a friend. Especially Rajamma considered her as another daughter.

Without bothering to get up, she called out to her mother and said, "*Amma…* Radhika is coming this evening." Rajamma replied, "Really? Glad she's coming, been so long."

That evening, as she was waiting, the doorbell rang. Sukrutha rushed in that direction and opened the door to find a slightly rounded Radhika and her cute son Balu. "Come, I was waiting for you," she welcomed her with excitement. The rest of the family appeared and wished her 'Hi'. Laughingly, Rajamma said, "Since morning, she has been jumping with excitement in anticipation of your coming." Somehow, Radhika did not talk much. Something else must be bothering her, thought Sukrutha. For a few minutes, they talked about worldly matters, and then Radhika approached Sukrutha and said in a hushed tone, "I want to talk to you about something in private." "So what, come…" she said. "Not here. In your room," said Radhika. Sukrutha took her to her room. On entering, Radhika did not look at Sukrutha but instead bolted the door. Sukrutha was surprised at Radhika's behaviour.

As they sat opposite each other, Radhika said, "Look, Sukrutha, I have come here to talk to you about something. Instead of talking about this and that and wasting time, isn't it better to get straight to the point?"

Sukrutha said, "What do you mean? Do you have to ask me like this?"

"You know everything about me anyway. I mean, you know that there's no relationship between me and him, meaning my husband."

"There's nothing to talk about. Let it go. What else?" said Sukrutha.

"Actually, for my Balu's sake, for his well-being, due to his persistence, because I was afraid that he would misconstrue the situation, I have done something without telling you," she said.

"Why do you have to tell me? Whatever you do for your child's well-being is your lookout," said Sukrutha.

"Let me be clearer. After that day's incident, you know the decision I took…"

"Yes, I know… and only you and I know about it," said Sukrutha.

"I spent a few years just like that, but I had to change it for Balu's sake. He insisted that he wanted his father and stopped eating or doing anything. He refused to go anywhere, created a ruckus, and cried all the time. Not just for a day or two. I got scared. That's why I had to do this. Meaning, he and I are together now," she said.

Sukrutha couldn't believe her ears. All her feelings burst out as if an unbearable weight was mounted on her head, as if everything in her grasp was escaping, as if she lost her tongue. She sat quietly with her eyes closed for some time. Then, she managed to calm her throbbing nerves. "Then, did you forget me completely? You completely ignored me as if whatever happened to me doesn't matter," she said in one breath.

Radhika observed the intensity of her feelings and said, "Not so. It's true that I have changed my decision and am living with him now. That's only because it will be good for my child. I don't want him to think that I am a bad mother. I just felt that things would work out this way. I'll repeat it again. In the eyes of society and family, we live under the same roof as husband and wife, and that's it. Everything is like before. I am on my own. He is on his own. Everything is separate to the extent that I have my room, and he has his. He has no entry into my room, day-night, anytime. We just pretend in front of Balu. We are acting well."

"I thought you had become weak," said Sukrutha. Unable to speak any further, she kept quiet for a few minutes.

"You have done all this for the child. For that, you are keeping yourself under control. That too for my sake, because my life was spoilt…" Sukrutha said, overcome with emotion.

Radhika held her hand comfortingly and said, "Don't become so emotional. Leave it be. Nobody can escape this situation. I did this only after coming to an agreement with him." She said. Then, they sat in silence for some time.

"I haven't just sat quietly. As I told you before, I've taken action," Sukrutha said.

Radhika, who felt happy hearing this, said, "Has there been any progress?"

Sukrutha sat silently again.

"Nothing so far. Must see from here on," she said after a pause.

Radhika held Sukrutha's hand and said, "Just one more thing…"

"What?"

"He is sitting in the car. Only if you grant permission, I will ask him to come here," she said.

Sukrutha felt a lightning run through her body. For a second, she was speechless, but then she recovered and said, "There's no need for everyone to know about this. Let us not make a big deal out of anything. Ask him to come in."

Radhika asked her husband to join them.

She said, "Let us keep this between us. He, too, should not know."

Later, they got up and came to the hall. Within a few seconds, her husband came. Sukrutha avoided eye contact when she invited him in. They spent some time having pleasant conversations with the other family members. Later, as Radhika was about to get into the car with her husband and son, she approached Sukrutha and said, "I hope you will give the good news very soon." Sukrutha replied, "I will certainly give it much sooner than you expect."

Sukrutha really appreciated Radhika's firm and justified decision. The same feeling enveloped her for a few days.

That day, she received an email from someone named Anand, who had shown interest in meeting her. Without delay, she replied, asking him to meet her the same evening if possible. As she got a confirmation from him, she worked cheerfully at the office until evening and left for the place at the time they had decided to meet.

She laughed at the thought that if her entire life had to be told briefly, it would only take a few seconds. The danger that she faced and the bitter experience kept haunting her mind. Yet, there was a ray of sunshine at a distance, giving her hope. As she turned, she saw that although the tree had shed most of its leaves, there were branches with some green leaves left on them. The heat strands that were spread out were reduced, and the pleasing cool breeze swirling around the flower petals brought about some joy. She spent a few minutes immersed in them.

When she reached, she realised that Anand had not arrived yet. He came within a minute or two. Since she recognised his face from the photo, she raised her hand slightly to wish him 'Hi'. As she saw him, she had a good feeling about him.

As he sat opposite her, she didn't feel like approaching the 'Conditions apply' right away. As usual, he started talking about mundane things, and they spent a few minutes with a clear mind.

Then he asked, "What are your conditions?" Based on the previous experience, she said, "Since marriage is a very intimate affair, I'm talking about the physical aspect that only the people who are getting married should be aware of…"

"I agree. Tell me your conditions," he said.

She went straight to the point and said, "Those who get married want their

life partner to be virgin."

Anand was a bit flustered as he felt that the talk suddenly crossed a line. On observing that, she reiterated to avoid any confusion and said, "Look, if you say that I'm right, isn't it natural for a man or woman to want the partner to be a virgin?"

He said, "Yes, everyone is like that."

"In case the partner is not a virgin, then there's no meaning to such a relationship."

"It is something to think about."

She said, "This is not in general… if it applies to us…" She looked up at him and said, "It's a simple matter. I am looking for someone who is not a virgin."

Now, he felt really lost. "What do you mean by that?" he asked.

She said, "I repeat that I'm not considering anyone without sexual experience. If you have had such an experience, we can continue our talk."

He looked at her with a keen eye and asked her in a serious tone, "If I were to ask you the same question, what would you say?"

To which she said, "Yes, I fulfill that requirement."

All of a sudden, he seemed to have drowned in his own thoughts.

As she observed that the talk had descended to silence, she said, "If that's the case, then I feel that there won't be any kind of issue, mental anguish, or any other unpleasant feelings."

He stared at her for a bit. Then he said, "What you say is one hundred percent correct. I will take a decision soon. Overall, I believe that this matter will resolve positively."

As soon as she heard what Anand said, she looked at him more keenly and said, "Then you mean to say you have had such an experience before?"

He simply nodded his head.

She said, "I will not ask for the details. I, too, would not like to share the details. In a way, as long as our situation is the same, that's enough."

She felt that this meeting was a lot smoother than the previous one, and opinions were exchanged without any hesitation.

"Then let us meet again at the earliest," he said.

They did not see the need to talk any further. They sat in silence for some time.

Later, as she said, "Shall we leave?."

"Oh yes."

They both got up.

She felt like she was floating gently as she stepped outside. Victory seemed to be embedded in the faces that she encountered.

As she returned home, she was happier to stay in silence. That way, she got the opportunity to talk to herself.

Anand called first thing in the morning. "Can we meet in the same place that we met, at the same time?" "No problem at all, let us meet," said Sukrutha. "I think everything will turn out fine," he hinted subtly that the meeting will be favourable.

The next day, she spent time until evening waiting to enter a new world. She wasn't herself at that time. She was yearning to take in all the goodness.

That evening, she went a little early and sat waiting for him. She called him after some time. The line was busy. When she called him again after a few minutes, there was no response from him. Soon after, she got a message from him, 'Will call you'. She continued to wait for him, thinking that he might be caught up in some urgent work. She became one with the minute needle of the ticking clock.

The Freedom

Dharani's daily routine is like an unchanged text for the past few years. She opens her eyes, springs out of bed and freshens up along with the first rays of the Sun. She draws the curtains and feels alive as the sunlight streams into the room. But Narayana continues to toss and turn in his sleep; she shakes his shoulders to wake him up and gets on with her routine work; this has become her habit. By this time, her slightly plump mother-in-law, Seethamma, attends to the pain in her knees, steps out to bring milk and curd after switching on the geyser, and prepares the coffee decoction. Then, with the remaining chores, the schedule is fixed. Each of them has their own things to do.

Seethamma's attention is focused on preparing breakfast and lunch with Dharani's help. Narayana is focused on reaching the cab's pick-up spot at least a few minutes ahead of time. He creates an island for himself and inevitably sinks into his laptop, working on the backlog from the previous day. Despite all this, he has to keep up with time. A man of medium build uses his hand gestures to convey what he wants; the tension in the air dissipates as soon as he picks up his bag and leaves for work. Then they are more relaxed.

The reason for this is the freedom that the fair-complexioned, slim Dharani enjoys from running her own dental clinic for the past two years. The attendee, Narasimha, takes care of opening the clinic every morning and doing other odd jobs. It does not take her long to reach the clinic, which is about three kilometres away. The clinic is situated in a prominent location, and people rarely miss seeing it. She comes home for lunch and then goes back only in the evening. Usually, they are all home for dinner, but sometimes Narayana returns home very late at night. At such times, silence reigns everywhere. It's also the time for the dim light and stale air at home to doze off. By then, Dharani's bright eyes have dimmed, and its bed time for Seethamma. They have come to accept his erratic working hours.

Seethamma's daily routine remains unchanged. True, there's a nagging pain in her knees. But without taking it to heart, she continues to work moving around the house; no job is too small for her. When told, "If you work without a break, the knee pain is sure to shoot up," she replies, "Does time stop ticking to take a break? It's only the mind that seeks rest. Let's see if the knee speaks up and asks for a break," making them laugh. She keeps trying out different kinds of medicine for her knee pain and regularly walks to the park, which is about half a kilometre from her house, without bothering about the effects of medicine. Half the purpose of going to the park is walking about twenty rounds there. The other half is catching up with friends and acquaintances. The bright-faced floral plants that swing with the wind in the park bear witness to all this. And the footprints on the ever-smiling walkway in the park mark her attendance for the day. Also, the smiles on the roadside shopkeepers' faces create a bridge of camaraderie along the way to the park. Dharani also accompanies Seethamma on some Sundays to add to the experience.

Of late, Dharani's mind is agitated- constantly swirling with thoughts; the minutes turn into hours as her mind wanders aimlessly in all directions. Everything around her slowly melts away, leaving her oblivious to all except her own self. It hits her with such great intensity that she is even unaware that her eyes are closed for a few seconds. Later, everything is itching to return to normalcy. She glances towards the clock only to avoid eye contact with Seethamma, who is getting ready to go to the park. She gives frivolous excuses for not joining her for the walk– she has to call her friend Sharmila, who is on hospital duty, or someone else. The usually decisive and firm Dharani is unable to accept the mix of both pleasant and unpleasant emotions in her mind. She immediately picked up the phone in order to avoid any possible suspicion that Seethamma might have had from the change of rhythm in her voice. But the soft wisp of wind that wraps her body finely is well aware of her state of mind and hides it. Seethamma is used to going alone at times like these.

"Now, the times have entirely changed. Not only the parks but all the shops, roadside vendors, and all other businesses are closed. Also, unless it's an emergency, people are restricted to their homes and are not supposed to step out. It's all about distancing. We cannot talk to our friends. It seems we must wear that thing called a mask. I feel that it resembles the scarf that thieves used to cover their faces at a crime scene during our times, in fact, even in today's movies. Also, I find it difficult to breathe when I wear it. It seems we have to stand at arm's length from one another. In such a situation, how can people who are hard of hearing manage? Unlike earlier, we cannot shake hands or whisper into each other's ears. Not only that, we just can't even touch babies anymore, let alone kiss them. Also, each one is suspicious if the other is infected with Corona. All that apart, where do we go if we contract some other disease? No idea what to do! Who will treat us for a minor cold and cough? Everybody is overcome with fear. Early in the morning, when we step out to fetch milk and curd, we have to wear that dreaded mask on our faces. A few times that I went without the mask, the milk vendor stood far away, as if he saw a snake, and asked me to leave the coupons there and pick up the packets. This keeps happening; what a fate! Corona, they say, is a virus that seems to be spreading every day. Also, every day, so many people succumb to it. I thought it would be a short sprint. What is the matter with this virus? That is one part. Especially when I think about the plight of those who have been infected, it sends shivers down my spine. What is that?.. Aah, yes, quarantine, it seems. That's a kind of jail- neither a hospital nor home. Not just for a day or two, they have to stay isolated for fourteen days or twenty-eight days, wherever they are told to, eating whatever food is given to them without complaining. Nobody, not even a family member, can stay with them. They just have to sleep quietly, it seems, without touching anyone and maintaining a distance of two arms' length from one another. Not only that, one after another, they go through many kinds of tests, it seems. *Rama Rama*!" said Seethamma, summarising all the happenings around her. She is not only upset about the closure of the park but the fact that the future is hazy and everyone is engulfed in fear and angst, something that she had never faced before. At the most, she had heard about similar situations from her parents. They had shared all the sights they had seen during the plague in their city- the innumerable deaths, the pain it had caused, and many more stories of agony. Will this discussion ever end? Everything around her is shrouded. She remembers how her parents had pulled her closer when they talked about people they had lost to the disease. But Corona beats that, too. She shares all the news that she watches on TV with the neighbours, as well as the news that she reads in the newspapers with her daughter Sugandhi over the phone. Now, she is fully aware of the virus taking over the world and its impact.

Narayana and Dharani also keep her informed. Despite the lockdown, Narayana barely has any free time. He holds a distinguished post in a prestigious software company and has to work from home now. He doesn't have to go to the office but remains glued to the laptop at home in his room with the door shut at all times. But weekends are all about relaxation. His office work disappears, and it is all about eating good food, snacks, laughter, and talk- lots of it! If he could fill sacks with his words, the whole house would be filled with these sacks, and they would have had to clear out the house just for that. Dharani almost becomes mute in response to his incessant chatter. She encourages him further by comparing his facial expressions, voice intonations, and other things to the lead actors in various dramas that she saw a long time ago. And the surrounding light and wind dance wildly around them.

In the last six to eight years, a few events have been close to Seethamma's heart. When her husband died in an accident, the feeling of emptiness and grief gave way to smiles during Sugandhi's wedding, then again when Narayana got a job, and finally during his wedding with Dharani. Even that was strange and special. It all started when Narayana went to watch a play. While waiting for his friend, he saw Dharani standing at a distance with a group of friends. He was mesmerised by the way she was analysing and criticising the subject and production of another play. Later, he got to know that Dharani's group was also waiting for the same person. That day's introduction culminated in marriage.

Outside the compound of the house, everything is tense. Due to the fatality of the virus and to curb the spread of Corona, the government has appropriately imposed a lockdown, although some rightly feel that it is an impulsive and unplanned move. Labourers, workers and migrants are left jobless with an uncertain future and without any means to get back to their native places too. All are worried about the pressures of living in the city and their inability to get back, resulting in a deadlock situation. Seethamma finds that even the street where they live has changed. People who have been living in the neighbourhood for ages look different, like strangers, walking with their masks on. It is much worse if they stop to talk. The voice that comes through the mask sounds robotic. Since many people warned her to do away with the house help, she is burdened with a lot more work at home now. On the other hand, Dharani is unable to attend her clinic because they have to close during the lockdown. So Dharani feels some kind of internal stress as she is forced to spend the whole day at home. Seethamma says, "If you get so upset just because you cannot go to the clinic, then how will you cope with the present situation?" For which she just forcibly laughs and says, "It is nothing of that sort." She doesn't want to tell her the truth. As soon as she leaves, Dharani closes her room door. Although she is often tempted to disclose the truth, she remains silent due to her state of limbo. She stands before the dressing table in the room and runs her hand over her stomach. Then she picks up the measuring tape from the drawer and checks her waist. She compares to see whether there's been any change in the past two weeks and becomes serious. Her eyes are half closed as she mulls. What if her mother-in-law realises and asks her, then what? Should she tell her the truth or lie about it, both are difficult for her. She is confused. Slowly, her blood pressure rises, and she sits down quietly. For the past few weeks, Narayana has been increasingly tormenting her.

When he comes into their room, she looks up at him, sensing a change in his gait.

"If you keep postponing it week after week, won't it become harder? If you do as I say our working conditions will definitely improve dramatically. Are you so stupid, don't you know that?"

"You only talk as convenient to you. Can't you think of anything else?"

"Tell me, what is more important than to improve our level at this point?"

"Is that the only important thing? If anybody is unable to understand this much, he must be called an idiot."

"You have given me a suitable title. Think fast and decide," he says sarcastically and walks out of the room.

She stands beside the window. It is scorching hot outside. The hot, blowing wind hits her face.

Seethamma returns home a little later that day after vegetable shopping. She appears to be fuming. As per practice, the vegetables are washed before use; she puts them away in a corner, rubs the sanitiser on her hands and says, "Why have people turned into *Rakshasas* (demons), the bastards? Is this even possible?" Dharani looks at her questioningly. "Why would anyone throw a newborn baby into the trash can? We live in such bad times. Why does one give birth? To throw out to the garbage? If they don't want it, they must take care to avoid it. Why sacrifice an innocent soul?" she says. "*Aiyoo*! Is that so? Was it still alive?" she replies, feeling a pinch inside her. "How is it possible? After wrapping in an old piece of cloth and throwing it away, what would be left? Such people must be caught and given the death penalty," Seethamma says fiercely. Dharani feels claustrophobic and unable to reply, so she turns her face away.

Lately, on some days, Dharani feels like it's too hot inside the house. That day, she knocks softly on Narayana's room door. As soon as he opens the door, she says, "Bring a thermometer to check the temperature." He replies, "Don't you know? We have one at home.Pull out the drawer, and you'll find it. Are you running a temperature?" She says, "Not the body, but I want one that can show the state of the mind, too." He glares at her and walks away. Later, she turns on the television to find only news on Corona and nothing else -- the details of the number of positive cases, deaths in Bangalore city and associated districts, the overall increase in the number of cases in the state, country and the world.

The doorbell rings. She sees the grocery delivery boy through the small window. As Dharani gets up to open the door, Seethamma says, "How can you open the door without wearing a mask? He just has it hanging around his neck. Tell him to wear it properly." After he leaves, Dharani puts the bags inside and rubs her hands with the sanitiser. Seethamma smiles at her.

Dharani does not see Narayana relenting on the issue.

"First, we must strengthen our base. The graph of our social status will rise upward, and we will start socialising and moving in the upper circles."

"For all this to happen, I must listen to you without another word, right?"

"I'm repeating the same thing to you over and over again."

"So what I have to say is not important?"

"Don't annoy me. We have already discussed this. You have agreed to pursue your master's. At the most, you may have to close your clinic."

"I think *Sahib* has forgotten when we discussed this and when I agreed to all this."

"I'm not crazy to forget. Are you testing me? Okay, it was soon after our first-year marriage anniversary. If my answer is correct, give me a ten on ten."

"Not relevant to the point. The number is a big zero."

"To hell with the number. Come to the point. Didn't you agree to everything? Don't evade the answer, and try my patience. You're really too much these days."

His face turns red as he walks away, and she steps out to find a lifeless and empty road.

She ponders. True. Earlier, she had agreed to his requests with great excitement; they had built dreams together. But what happened? Her, also, their plans had gone awry unexpectedly. But is it possible to reject the current situation, that too, for such materialistic reasons? It is difficult to believe that he doesn't understand that. Also, he is pressurising her. It is difficult to decide whether it is his stupidity or impudence.

"Look, try to understand just this once. If I don't want it now, it doesn't mean that I will never want it. Can't we make proper plans once we are settled?" he says in a placating voice.

She finds herself thinking about him. He might be thinking that I'm a fool to try all this. What does he mean by saying we will take care of it sometime in the future when everything is in place? Everything is in our control, he says. The arrogance that we can shape our life however we want. But at present, he implies that it must be sacrificed. What can one say to that? Is he stupid enough not to know who is stupid? *Che! Che!*

That day, when Dharani felt a change in her body, she went to Sharmila's nursing home for a check-up. Narayana had not accompanied her as he had some meeting. After the examination, instead of revealing the results, Sharmila pinched Dharani's cheeks. "*Ammayya*, give me a grand treat," she had said and laughed. Dharani felt bursts of rainbow glowing all over her. She couldn't wait to share the news with Narayana. It was a silver lining to the shining light. Even as the ground tickled her feet, her mind raced to the stars in the sky. On returning home, she had waited for Narayana to take a break from his work, beckoned him to meet her alone, and then shared the news. "Is that so?" he had asked, his eyes wide with wonder, diving deep into her eyes. Only she knew how much she had anticipated that moment. His excitement had mingled with hers. But now she doesn't understand how his thoughts have changed so much within a few months. 'Instead of telling this now, if only he had made it clear to me earlier, we could have planned perfectly,' she thinks, gazing at him. "My calculations were right," he says in a low tone. "So what? There is always a way out," he says, raising his voice and not meeting her eyes. "True, there is. But you must look at it as a whole. Then you'll know," she says.

Dharani's mind wandered to Narasimha. Narasimha, who had migrated to the city, had joined her clinic as a helper after being referred by someone known to her. Other than telling her the name of his birthplace and parents, he never talked nor wanted to reminisce about his childhood days. But some time back, he disclosed to her that he came from a poor family. His father worked as an honest accountant in a rich man's shop, and his integrity brought his downfall when he was wrongly accused of stealing money, and everything spiralled out of control. Narasimha's studies had come to a full stop in the tenth standard. Also, when his peers teased and berated him, he ran away from home, deciding never to set foot in that city, and came straight to her. That turned out to be a gift from the unknown to her. If his father had been a man of integrity, he was a notch above! She had given him a room to stay in the clinic itself. Also, he would remember the ailment of every patient, the treatment given, and their progress during their consultation without writing anything down. During lockdown, there's just silence when he closes the clinic; when he opens the clinic doors, he sees only the deserted street, the passing shadows, and the stray dogs that are fast asleep even at noon. Initially, he had said, "TV is very interesting…" Lately, he says, "TV is very boring…"

Gurupadappa, who had helped her get the place, was known to her right from her college days. The revenue officer had appreciated her performance in a play. In that, she had played the part of a leader of a movement who opposed animal sacrifice to appease the goddess for selfish needs. He had said, "It was good, but it would have been even better if you had included infant sacrifice that people do in the name of some goddess or the other." Recently, he had formed a group of people who were sympathetic towards the workers and labourers who suddenly lost their jobs due to the lockdown and decided to distribute kits of essential food items. He had made arrangements to distribute it in a high school that was under his supervision. Even before he asked Dharani for help, she said, "There's no need to ask, sir." She had also excitedly asked him to include her contribution to the kits. The interaction with those people at that time had left her parched. She often relived the picture of countless people who looked beaten and lost, wearing tattered clothes with helpless faces, standing, looking up with extended hands.

When Dharani had told Seethamma about the kit distribution, she said, "What? Are you going as well? Please be careful. You may meet all kinds of people. It's ok if they are hungry, but people with this deadly illness may come there. We should be careful, right?" Dharani replied reassuringly, "No. No. We have made all arrangements." Narayana had shown a lot of excitement about it. Also, he said, "That's great. But hope you remember your condition. You may forget it in that hustle and bustle." She smiled and said, "How is that possible? That's the first priority." On the day of the distribution of kits, she had felt very special. Her mind and body had felt very light, as though heavy sacks of worry in her mind were thrown out, as though her feet were floating above the ground.

She had asked Narasimha to accompany her that day. He was bubbling with excitement. He believed that it was very special for him to be a part of such a program. He had tried to stop people from coming close to the kits and reduce their clamouring. Although Gurupadappa had been a bit upset by the people's behaviour and indiscipline, he said, "They are our own people. They just have to behave a little bit better. That's all." After that day's program, he told everyone about his plans to meet again. Fifteen days later, a similar program took place, and everything was under control. Those who had participated exchanged smiles while they did the assigned jobs. When she told Seethamma about this, she had asked, "Hope you are still feeling strong and well? You had got them all tested- yes or no?" Without saying much, she had just nodded her head to satisfy her, laughing to herself because it was impossible to do all that, nor could they afford it. Narayana did not want her to go despite her pleas. "You're just too much. If something had gone wrong, who would be answerable? Now that it's done, you must not go for such programs anymore. Got it?" he had scolded her.

That morning, Narayana wakes up very late. Dharani is aware that he does that when he has no work pressure. Although he usually watches TV while eating or drinking, that day, he quietly takes a cup of coffee from Dharani. When she herself picks up the TV remote to turn it on, he stops her. With a low and serious tone, talks as if narrating a dialogue in a play; Narayana says, "You haven't yet made a decision, but time is running out. Can't wait anymore. Primarily in your interest…" She reduces the volume of the TV and says a bit harshly, "Why so early in the morning? I know. I'll tell you." She sees him frown and says, "Doesn't it have to be in both our interests?" She walks away without waiting for his reply. His pressure of settling everything within the stipulated time bothers her. She is unsure if working in a big company after her MD would really bring her accolades. She also suspects that she may not have the freedom in a big firm, which she enjoys now. Most importantly, she just does not like being forced to end the life of the one growing in her stomach in order to get this.

She wonders how to make him toe the line when he is so one-sided. If she adheres to his wishes, how would she be any different from those who sacrifice their babies in semi-darkness? Killing a foetus that is yet to open its eyes in an operation theatre is no different from what happens in the shadow of darkness. How can he not see that? Lately, he has been shooting arrows of a different kind. Earlier, he would just sit with a grumpy face, but now he gives her a knowing look, gives some excuse to his mother, and says, "I don't want lunch today." Being totally ignorant, she says, "But it was prepared specially for you." To which he replies, "Why didn't you ask me before preparing it?" It is difficult to see him play such games without reason. Her mind fixates on his behaviour. He thought that I would surrender and agree to his terms. That made me angrier. The next day, mother-in-law gave him a bigger breakfast. He didn't pursue the topic that day, so she couldn't guess. The following day, once again with a smile, he asked, "What does *ammavru* say?" for which I frowned and said, "Which play is this dialogue from?" Whatever it is, I feel that I can handle this easily. But he did the most unexpected and hurtful thing of all. "Unless you do as I say, I will not talk to you," he said curtly; I thought that he was joking. But he was very serious about it. I had not expected something so extreme. He probably imagined that I'd melt within two days and fall at his feet. This seems to be the greatest challenge to me. Since both of us are adamant, we have ignored the crux of the situation. I've begun to feel terribly anxious and stressed. I am sad that our relationship has come down to this level. I cannot sleep even late into the night. I worry that it is also affecting my health. But he pretends like nothing has happened and begins his routine work in the morning. He expects me to give in very soon. But I feel like he is becoming stronger to brace his new arrows. It is surprising how all these changes are not visible on the outside. But the surrounding light and air, the sofa, chairs, TV and other things at home don't feel the same. They sense the tension and look questioningly at me.

She remembers her clinic and all the things there, especially Narasimha. Even without any traditional relationship, how did this lad get so close to her? She is amazed at how a destitute like him overcame so many obstacles and progressed in life. She feels impressed and proud of the way he paints himself and his life in a different way. A silent smile peeks at the corner of her lips and spreads across her face. She gets up and switches on the TV. On watching the news of the migrants' struggle to get back to their hometowns and the news of the headlong behaviour of the leaders for media and popularity, she switches it off. As she steps outside, she feels that the heat has gone up. She wishes that it would increase by a hundred times and consume her.

Just then, the mobile rings. It is Narasimha. "Please come right away, madam. It is very urgent. Someone is here and has been suffering since they got here. Can't even describe the pain of the people who have accompanied her," he says without stopping to take a breath. Finally, he says, "Please come immediately, madam, she appears to be pregnant, full term. Those who have accompanied her are worried." She is shocked! The one who came to her clinic was a full-term pregnant woman. But it's a dental clinic, a place to treat dental issues. She has studied and practised the same. And now there's a lady in labour! She has never delivered a baby before. Should she tell Narasimha the same and ask them to go elsewhere? She chastises herself for having such thoughts. For some reason, she does not want to quietly accept defeat. She takes a few deep breaths and then decides to figure it all out in the clinic and leaves. As she approaches her clinic, she finds a small gathering there. She grasps the seriousness of the situation even from a distance. As she approaches, Narasimha says, "I told them many times, they refused to pay heed. They pleaded and said, isn't she a doctor? She can help; please call her." The pregnant woman's sounds of suffering reverberate with his words. Dharani has no time to think. Pairs of vacant, helpless eyes beseech her to take up a task she has never done before. All the nerves in her body and mental strength remind her that she is a doctor, after all. Although unexpected, she closes her eyes for a few seconds, praying for strength to face the current situation. Then, she braces herself to perform the procedure, face the outcome and follow all the necessary steps.

Dharani does not talk to any of the men or women standing with the pregnant woman. She assures the woman, "Don't be afraid; I'm here. Everything will be fine." The woman looks perplexed and turns towards a woman standing beside her. She tells her what she presumes, in Hindi, "*Shayad keh rahi hai sab kuch theek ho jayega* (She is probably saying that all will be well.)". That's when Dharani realises that they do not know Kannada. Then, she gestures and communicates with them in broken Hindi. First, she points at the pregnant woman and asks them to bring her in. She gestures and says, "*Usko andar le aiye* (Bring her in.)" Then the women who are with her bring a few sarees. She uses them to create walls around her. Then, she becomes immersed in the work, instructing them.

Even as she is engrossed with work, one of the men keeps talking to Narasimha. The meaning of his words is this: When we were waiting to go back to our native place in Bihar, we were made to stand in line with many others and went through thermal screening. Then, one of the authorities there had forced the pregnant woman and two others to get quarantined. No matter what we said about our difficulties and the pregnant woman's misery, they did not listen. Finally, they had chanced upon a higher authority who found out that the other officer had made a mistake. So they let us go. Otherwise, we would have been struggling out there. Nobody would have heard us out, especially the pregnant woman's condition would have been pathetic. What to do? Then we roamed around the streets in search of a hospital, with her crying out in pain. Someone had pointed in the direction of this hospital. We decided to try, no matter what. We found you, and the lady doctor also came. Else, she may have been in a terrible state. We will always be indebted to her.

Dharani is confident despite the pressure. She manages to perform and complete the entire procedure with the instruments that she has, from cutting close to the navel to delivering the baby. The surroundings become clear. She performs the fairly simple procedure for normal delivery without much effort. The other women clean up the room after delivery. Once things become stable, she gazes unblinkingly at the mother and baby for a few seconds. She begins to wonder. How happy is the mother, and how happy was she? If the new mother's pain is of one kind, what kind was her own pain? Is it possible to list it out? The women take turns holding the baby and say, "*Bahut naseeb ka bachcha* (Very lucky baby.)," "*Kya kehna bol nahi sakte* (Don`t know what to say)." They express their happiness and admiringly look at the baby and then at Dharani, nodding their heads and laughing. The men pat each other's shoulders gently.

All the men and women gathered there race each other eagerly to fall at her feet and seek her blessings. "*Arre! Yeh kya kar rahe ho* (Hey, what are you doing?)?" Narasimha says in Hindi, over and over again, trying to stop them. They ignore his words. She is terribly embarrassed. After their job is done, they all stand in groups and discuss their next move. The sounds of the street begin to come alive. In the midst of all this, Dharani slips away into isolation. The path she had taken in the past, her experiences, hopes and thoughts roll before her eyes. Now she sees a huge scary demon before her. She is scared like a little rabbit. Slowly, she gathered courage from her recent experience. As she relives it, the demon becomes smaller and smaller. Finally, he becomes a small newborn infant in her hand. Happily, she gets up and walks towards the baby. What she carries in her hand becomes one with the baby. Now everything is crystal clear; everything now has a new shade, and hope is reborn. She is ready with her decision. Without further delay, she picks up her mobile phone to call Narayana.

The Park

*S*umathi wondered how a fitful sleep after a day of stressful work passed by so quickly. She still had to get ready for the morning routine. Even as she got up from bed, the rays of light penetrating through the gaps between the blue curtains of the eight-foot-wide window appeared to be struggling not to lose their intensity. As she stood still for a second, admiring them as if to placate them, a list of essential tasks for the day overpowered her. The amount of time they spent together had to be limited. It was imperative that the balance sheet be cleared of all the work that needed to be accomplished, switching on the boiler and then fetching the milk and curd, along with all the work that had to be done parallel to preparing breakfast and lunch. Just a few years ago, Nagaraja used to wake up with her and help her with the morning chores. At present, it was all in her godown of memories. Nagaraja woke up only in time to complete his morning routine like clockwork. She would announce that the coffee was ready as soon as she heard him move, and then he proceeded to wash and wipe his face, silently grabbed the cup of coffee, sat down on the sofa, and took out his laptop even as he kept an eye on the time. As she cooked, she could easily predict what Nagaraja would be doing in the following moments. Then, she would hurriedly get on to her prepping work. Rarely did Nagaraja realise that she, too, must get ready along with him. As if to prove that this was normal, the bond between them went beyond any talk. In the conversation between their gestures and eye contact, even the strands of words are missing the fun, petty quarrels, anger, smiles, and so on, which bring about many different expressions that go out of the boundary.

It was known even before their marriage that both were software employees. Suppose she left for the office at eight o'clock, he at nine. If this was a difference in their timings, there was also a difference in the way they worked as well as the stresses that went with it. They also sat down with a questionnaire to find out more about this in detail after a sumptuous meal. They even took several additional papers to write. However, on evaluation, they only got a row of zeroes. In the end, they had just looked at each other and laughed. In the beginning, all such activities made them fly strange colourful kites and the laughable desire to see if they could climb as high. If she tried to count on her fingers, the time that had passed since they shared such days, instantly, all the fingers would stick together and become one. The counting hangs.

There were no such knotty issues at her office. There, bridges were built for a few seconds as she conversed with some of her colleagues. Just before they disappeared, a curiosity was born from the way the eyes met. Often, the eyes appeared to have hidden waves of thoughts which had nothing to do with the present work. That gave rise to a curiosity to look into those dreams deep in their eyes. Many times, she felt a deep desire to know whether it was related to their career or a personal sphere. Even as she saw the colourful lines coming together to form a figure, it would immediately vanish. The perception was stunted. The rising smile faded. Not only that, she had also wondered how to look for the strands of pain hidden deep in the eyes of the boy who brings coffee on time at the office. In addition, she had her office work. There were times when the nerves were pulled and tied from one peg to the other and tested to find the spot where it made a distinct tune. But Sumathi knew that she wasn't the only one facing this. This was just the usual everyday rain. Even as she tried to figure out how much of this was useful and how much had gone down the drain, the corners of her eyes were set on the passing hours and days to the Saturday-Sunday. Only then did she crave to get rid of all that was office-related. Whatever the case, she had wilfully watered, nourished and cultivated a habit. While getting in and out of the office, she would plant her gaze at the park spread out all along the office compound wall, full of green and flowery plants to fill her eyes. She had a great desire to absorb this sight deep within her. She would stand with her eyes closed for a few seconds and then step forward.

Sumathi was not unaware that Nagaraja was also in a similar circle at work. It was not a lie that, as a newlywed couple, they would discuss the antics of their colleagues and bosses, laughing out loud. They felt that the entire world belonged to them during the weekends. They spent a lot of time figuring out how to use the time piled up before them. On top of the list was the hotel where they wanted to have breakfast, followed by the other places they wanted to visit. They would be ready even before the housekeeper finished her work, their eyes fixed on the ticking seconds. Sometimes, Sumathi stood outside the house, marvelling at how the bright sunlight could create such wonder. "You are very right…" he would stop a while and say, "Try if possible… maybe we can store a little bit of this light at home" and proceed to take the car out. At such times, she would modify and hum one of Purandhara Dasa's songs, *'Ee pariya sobagu innaava oorinali kaane…'* ('I haven't seen such beauty in any other city…') loud enough for Nagaraja to hear. As she did that, she said, "In my childhood, my mother found a music teacher for me since I was interested in Carnatic music. When one of her friends heard about it, she said, 'Oh, that man… right… he doesn't put the *taala* (beats) on his own lap… instead on one of the innocent girls sitting there to learn the lessons…' and covered her mouth with the edge of her saree. My mom broke into a cold sweat and stopped my lessons immediately. Otherwise, I would have been a *vidushi* (master singer)." Once they reached the road, she was usually monosyllabic. When she had the urge to listen to music, she would play *keeerthane* rendered by her favourite Chembai Vaidyanatha Bhagavathar, Balamuralikrishna, Subbulakshmi, Sudha Raghunathan or Bombay Jayashree from a pen drive; and closed her eyes, immersed in it. If they reached the hotel when the song was playing mid-way, she would look disappointed. In the later years of her childhood, her mother realised that she loved flowers as much as music. She would also tease her about it. But when she felt that Sumathi's interest was quite extreme, she said, "If you continue this, I'll just get you married to a flower vendor." For which, she would make a long face and reply, "I don't want that… it's fine as long as there's a park like the one on the way to school." Clueless, her mother would say, "I'll do that," making her jump with joy. With dancing eyes, when she narrated this to Nagaraja, he said, "You and your mother are just too much." When she replied, "Then you would have got zilch," he said, "Is it so easy... how would I let go of this *Padmavati*..." as he wrapped his arm around her waist and pulled her closer. As he remembered all that, he tried to lightly poke her with his finger. She said, "You better keep your eyes on the road, *Saheb*..." and scooted a little farther. Then they reached Gandhi Bazar as pre-decided. The broad road there was lined with many trees with overflowing greenery and an abundance of soft shade. As they left 'Vidyarthi Bhavan', after appreciating the enthusiastic waiter who balanced several plates of dosas in each hand and served with a smile, the shade on the streets seemed a bit heavy. After spending the whole day out and returning back home, they'd wonder how quickly the day had passed. This was the usual practice. Sometimes, she would be caught in the intense emotions she felt for music and the colourful flowers in the park and celebrate; that was apparent in the way she spoke. He was baffled by her posture as her sole touched the floor. He was like a stranger, unable to touch her state of mind.

When they started working, they lived in a rented house in the centre of the city. Since it topped the list due to the ease of commuting to their work, they liked the place. Gradually, that excitement began to wane. They began to face many problems in that house. It was tiring to just go to the dairy booth, grocery shop and the iron shop. Sometimes, they would not only struggle to get vegetables, but often, when the ATMs would become paupers, they looked miserable. On the other hand, electricians and plumbers would usually speak in Telugu or Tamil, and their priority was to first check whether they knew Kannada. Above all, the surroundings were extremely dirty. There was such a bad odour that they had to cover their noses when moving about.

There was absolutely no question of flowers. Only after entering the house and closing the doors could they sniff and smell the jasmine or champaka flowers; she was overcome with anger at this situation, and her throat felt parched as if she was barely alive. He could sense her anguish immediately and would place his palm on her shoulders to pacify her. Sometimes, to tease her, he would pick up the flowers one at a time and place them near her nose, only to infuriate her further. Why, even the weekend excitement lasted only as long as they were out of the house.

She had to walk some distance, then take the Metro and then again walk for a bit to reach her office. When they were newly married, Nagaraja would forcibly drop her to the station. Later, over time, it reduced, and at present, there is no sign of that. During such times, she walked hurriedly, half stiff and half burnt. Then, the morning breeze was her companion. It would caress her ears and eyes back to normalcy. As she sat in the metro, with her eyes closed, pulling out everything from the treasury of her memories, the pictures that brought comfort earlier seemed to have faded and stumbled in the race. Sometimes, she was shrouded in doubt whether that face she saw was her own. On other days, when she smoothly completed all the morning chores without any kind of variation in her heartbeat, and the Sun rays warmed her heart, the Metro felt like a *Rajahamsa* (flamingo). On such days, she captured her copassengers' facial features, glow, and the movement of muscles as they talked; she clicked a mental picture of all this and sat with her eyes closed. Those faces created a variety of colourful flowers in her mind.

Just to escape from those surroundings, they moved to a second-floor apartment in a new locality. It made them feel very secure.

Nagaraja's colleague Divya was instrumental in this. On many occasions, he had expressed Divya's views on the importance of a person's interests, outlook, the ability to showcase and the courage one must have for it, rather than a person's education, career, salary, and so on. During such times, he did not look straight into her eyes. Sumathi would make up excuses for that and kept quiet. Once, unable to bear it any longer, she asked teasingly, "What is it? You seem to turn your face to the sky whenever her name comes up?" He replied, "No… no… nothing great about her. Maybe she's just slightly different, that's all. Other than that, she is like any other person," and avoided her gaze. She would then remain quiet for a few minutes, as if in agreement with him, and then again continue teasing him on the same topic, "Ask that shining Divya to visit us once… some light will shine in this dull house…" for which, he replied, "Sure… Why just the house? We will get enough light to awaken our minds also guaranteed…" He would laugh and change the topic to changing their house and make her happy. "That's not so urgent… but if she's really coming, ask her to bring a park along with her," she said, leaving him confused.

That day, when the doorbell rang, she opened the door to find a middle-aged man with a lady of approximately her own age who said, "I'm Divya… Mister Nagaraj…" She heard nothing beyond those words. In that split second, she gave Divya a look over and processed it in her mind. True, Divya's figure was not as attractive as her own. But she felt that Divya's attractive eyes shone like a mobile's flash. She had come with her middle-aged cousin, who worked in real estate and so on, to show them a house. Nagaraja said, "If you had informed us earlier, we would have been ready." Divya replied, "I did this only to surprise you." He said, "Understandable… true to your nature." Then, there was no break to her tongue. She talked about all her mutual friends and colleagues, spreading out all the information and ironing it. When she started talking about their boss, Nagaraja, who had been adding to her words until then, was clean-bowled and said, "We had discussed it long back anyway," and reminded her of the work in hand. Sumathi was amazed and jealous of the varying tempo of Divya's talk.

On the way to see the house, the man said, "Although it is close to the main road, we must go round the block… since there is a park…" These words made Sumathi extremely happy. "Is there a park near the house?" Even as she said this, her spirit soared high. She didn't hear any of the talk in the car about office, locality and so on. They had instantly decided to take the house on the second floor. The main reason was the fairly large park that was visible from the hall window. It was full of green plants and trees, and the spread of multi-coloured flowers had tied a *thorana* (decorative door hanging) to her mind. She ignored the others and just stood, looking at it. Nagaraja was enquiring about the small adjustments that they may have to make to live in that house. Sumathi didn't say much. Divya observed this and finally said, "Looks like your *missus* really likes this house. The fact that she is quiet is proof." Only then did Sumathi turn to look.

Nagaraja did not know that by changing the house, Sumathi would behave as if every day, the doors were decorated with *thorana* of various fresh green leaves and colourful flowers. In just a few days after shifting into the new house, he realised that when she had said, "I am very, very happy. Thanks a lot," to

Divya on the day of shifting, it wasn't just a formality. She had the same excitement and enthusiasm as the days when they were newlywed. It resurfaced in the form of the shirt, its colour, shoes matching pants and many other ways. Nagaraja also tried to react with matching intensity. Also, he just got an inkling of the reason behind Sumathi's overall heightened state of mind and body. He didn't have the heart to tease her about it. He suspected that it would put a brake on her. There were new colours of excitement in their daily routine work from the moment they woke up to the sweet indulgence of togetherness at night and everything else. He didn't feel the need to ask her anything since everything was becoming clear, even without words. This made him feel younger. Nagaraja did not keep this feeling to himself. He shared it happily with Divya. As a reply, she had just given him a look sharp enough to kill. Nagaraja, too, got a glimpse of the strands of desires that were circling deep in her mind.

That day, at lunch, as he was sharing lunch with her and two other colleagues, he suddenly announced, "Your attention, please… Divya would like to share her plans of marriage…" The clear air had suddenly become thick as Divya pushed the lunch box away and got up, saying, "Who told you this? Very, very naughty…" for which Nagaraja said, "Take it easy…" and consoled her.

Usually, Nagaraja would reach home only at the time after the roads were yawning, tired and ready to lie down to sleep. But Sumathi, who would reach home when it was still somewhat bright, would rush to the park the very next day after shifting to the new house. Her intention was to spend as much time there as possible. If she tried to express in words the difference between her experience when looking through the window of her house and her experience when she actually stood there and looked around, it wasn't easy. Especially the first time she went there; she was floating all day. The different flowers, plants-trees-climbers grew according to their individuality. Not only the outer beauty but the fragrance emanating from the rows of blooming flowers and the special tunes were pulling her. Not only did she grasp their combined essence in her fist, but also a handful and enjoyed it. She turned into a new person right there. As she danced back and looked at herself in the dressing table mirror, she said to herself, 'Who is she?'. She raised her eyebrows admiringly and said, 'Wah!' She was thrilled to have discovered something new about herself. When Nagaraja came home, he was unable to understand her state of mind and felt lost. That day, all that he got was beautiful and new. She went into a trance, especially when she heard the song written by K. S. Narasimhaswamy, sung by M. Prabhakar, 'Hakkiya haadige thaledooguva hoo naanaaguva aase…' (I wish to be the flower that nods its head and listens to the song of the birds…). Later, she gently stroked the nearby flower. That night, she tried to share her feelings with Nagaraja. He just snubbed her excitement by saying, "I'm first. Then the park." She went pale at his sharp words. He was usually not the type to get so agitated so easily. She wondered what else could be the reason.

The next day, when Sumathi went to the park, she was a lot calmer. All the waves in her mind had even out, and she was not in a hurry to grab everything and stuff it all in. Even the park appeared to have the intention of working hard to please people's minds. Although the entire park was gloriously green, the flowering plants were also luscious. Then, there were also the usual stone benches and other things neatly laid out in the park. There were men, women and children of different ages everywhere. Sumathi walked slowly, absorbing everything. She could hear music from the speakers all along the walkway.

That day, for some unrelated issue, he had raised his voice and said, "You and your park… the plants and flowers there… the chitchat… this-that is just nothing… talk about it to the babies…" As she heard it, she shivered as though her insides were being squeezed. She stood still and stared hard at him, piercing every part of his face.

As days passed, Sumathi felt as if the entire park was within her. Since she would usually see the same faces there every day, their friendship grew and bloomed quickly. Housewife Lakshmi, school teacher Vasavi, bank employee Vimala and others. She inspired them by talking about how they could make the park even more beautiful than it already was. Adding a wider variety of flowering plants, colourful decorations, electric lights, children's playground and more. Sumathi grew wings when she was in charge of getting the work done within a stipulated time. Among her friends, Vimala had two cute young children. Although she had a very good time with them, she felt troubled that she and Nagaraja were not seriously trying or planning for a baby. She spent the next two to three days planning to talk to Nagaraja about this and make a decision. These days, it was as if he had lost his tongue, but as he observed Sumathi's curved eyebrows pulling each other and growing shorter, he said, "What *ammavru*… looks like you have a *sakkath* (heavy) load on your head. Just say yes. I'll take a look at it." She had just been waiting for words from his mouth and replied, "How much longer can we just live this way… just the two of us." He said, as if he didn't understand,

"Meaning?" "What else? Don't you have ears and eyes? Isn't it true that we are throwing away old calendars every year?" she said, not wanting to explain it all to him. "Oh, is that it… I don't think that is such an emergency issue," he said. He got up from there and picked up his laptop. He was surrounded by an island of light. She was sitting on her knees on the bed. He returned to bed after a long time, stared at her for a split second and fell asleep beside her. He woke up as usual the next morning. She was still sitting on the bed. Without a word, he got ready for office and left. Only when the househelp called her she pushed aside the various types of shadows that surrounded her.

That night, they had fought over some trivial issue until their throats were parched. There was no scope for the outside world to peep in. There was no entry for the soothing breeze that could excite the minds or the light from the shining street lamps that were thrilled to have just touched the ground. Let alone talking, they turned away from each other to avoid looking at each other, splashed some food on their plates, swallowed it, and slept facing away from each other. That's when Sumathi decided. 'I will not remind him about tomorrow. Let him open his mouth first.' In the morning, the hands in the watch kept ticking, but he was just as usual. Sumathi was seething with anger. As the time passed, she was stressed. As she got ready and crossed the doorway, she turned around and looked at him and sobbed. As he lifted his head up, she said, "Didn't you even realise… isn't it our anniversary today?" Without waiting to hear his reply, she walked away.

Sumathi came across more people due to her work at the park. Even at work, there were many times when she had to talk to her colleagues about the park, and they were all aware of this. Some of them, either to tease her or to show their appreciation, gave her a nickname - park. "How are you, Park?" "Welcome Park…" and she too laughed with them. And in her neighbourhood, she became "Park madam".

Although Nagaraja was well aware of this development, he just put it aside as if it wasn't anything great. He began to feel that she was gaining more trust and affection from many people. Also, people who visited would look crestfallen if she wasn't home and would leave without another word. Not only that, on several occasions, he had heard people referring to him as 'Isn't that Sumathi's husband?' and had a heated argument with her on that count. "Am I just Sumathi's husband? Don't I have anything else?" for which she had said, "What do you get by asking me this… Ask them…" And when he had begun to raise his voice, she placed her finger on her lips and hushed him as if to say, "Don't create a scene. If you do, you will face trouble." This made his face burn as if all the burners of the stove were lit up at once.

Sumathi was stunned when Nagaraja brought the park between them. She had understood Nagaraja's mind and had wholeheartedly appreciated and accepted him with his beliefs and character, and so she married him. She strongly believed that he, too, did the same. Just like the elders, didn't she set up a household with Nagaraja believing that marriage was togetherness or a happy relationship and that she was only working for mutual harmony? Otherwise, she sometimes felt that, without the shackles of marriage, they probably lived together now with the mindset of a "live-in" relationship. This made her laugh a little. On one side was the old-fashioned social marriage, which sought the blessings of everyone. Then, the extreme anxiety that their overall mindset, flashes of their individuality, nature, the future and other things that determined the quality of their life together seemed to be vanishing. This spread the full moonlight in her mind. But now, all this feels like a long time ago. Lately, whenever she thought of herself and Nagaraja, she and the park, she worried whether there was a sufficient match between Nagaraja and her behaviour. She was hounded by the feeling of whether they had moved from a 'live in' kind of a relationship to the 'live out' kind. Of late, she was perturbed that not only Nagaraja's expressions but even during moments of intimacy when his body must be hot, his eyes were vacant. Their talk went beyond the obvious meaning. The differences between them peeked in the lines that appeared between his eyebrows. She begins to feel it's absurd to even wonder why this is happening. She was surprised when some flowers in the park began to look like commas, while some creepers looked like question marks when she took a walk. It was only natural that they had begun to create their own separate worlds due to all this, she thought.

As expected, Nagaraja was promoted to group manager in the same office. It was decided that they must throw a party on that count. Nagaraja knew that she would attend the party. But she had the job of deciding on four to five locations in the park to install the steel fabricated arches and coloured light bulbs around them. Due to this, she couldn't go. She didn't do it on purpose. Nagaraja also knew that her programme had been set earlier, yet after a few days, he blamed her in front of a few friends. When she did not retort back, he felt more powerful and also raised his voice. His friends just wished him and left in a hurry to avoid any further embarrassment. But Nagaraja felt proud of winning.

They would invite their colleagues home several times for breakfast or for a slideshow of the photos that they took during jolly rides or outings that they went on together. The main topic during those times was the office. When everyone talked mainly about that, Sumathi would begin to talk incessantly about the park even if they turned their face away. Lately, they had almost stopped coming, unlike before.

People at the flat were aware of this, and they were also familiar with Divya, who visited the flat. Recently, when one of them met Sumathi, he said, "Are you not well, madam… you didn't come to watch the movie. I'm only asking since only Divya accompanied your husband." She replied, nothing of that sort. I'm fine. I was just busy with some other work." Nagaraja did not come home that day and again later for a day or two. Even when he came later, Sumathi did not ask him anything. Although Nagaraja was surprised by this, he felt that it was only convenient for him, and he tried to talk to her and help out with the household chores more than necessary. Sumathi laughed to herself. Then life went on as usual as if nothing had happened. But it could not continue for long. When he stopped coming home regularly, Sumathi asked, "I'm not sure whether you will come home or not… and I won't know where you will be… let me know whatever that is… "He replied, "You know everything, what's more to say?"

As she stepped into the park, she felt like the flowers that had bloomed just that morning invited her with a melodious song. It's true that sometimes she felt wistful for not having enough knowledge of music to identify the exact *raga* (tune) and *bhaava* (emotions) with each of the different coloured flowers. But her face would brighten up as a voice seemed to whisper that it isn't enough for the emotions to touch you, irrespective of the tune. She would then rush towards the flowers. She was thrilled to see the mild rays of sunlight delightfully touch the beautiful flowers as per the season. Also, some dew drops emanated several colours as they adorned the flower petals and made her heart leap. People were amazed at her ability to identify each flower and the date when it was seen. She was always plagued by one question whether it was possible to determine when the fragrance takes birth in these flowers. But then she realised that it's better to enjoy it rather than understand the minute details of the way nature works. This way, she absorbs a little here and a little there, and finally, the entire park within herself. The gentle laughter of the walkers in the park only mingles with all this, whereas their low voices scatter away. In all this excitement, her mind did not register whether Nagaraja came or did not come home.

That day, she saw Divya's cousin, who had come to show them the flat, with a few other people. He was holding a tape and measuring something in the park. Sumathi approached him and said, "Do you remember? You are the one who showed us our house, right? What are you doing?" He just laughed in response and continued to talk to the people with him, wrote something down and left. Maybe as a result of meeting him or something, she soon heard that they were destroying the park to widen the main road. She felt like she was standing on burning coal. Although she immediately got in touch with the concerned authorities, she did not get any response from them. She thought that it was probably not true. Yet, she got some banners against the destruction of the park and hung them in a few places. She also ensured that the houses in the neighbourhood displayed messages to save the park.

Perhaps as a result of this, there was no activity or news regarding this for a few days.

Sometimes, Sumathi would often stand and stare as if she were assessing the flowers and leaves of a single plant. The flowers and leaves in any bunch were not exactly identical. As she observed that even the branches of one tree twisted and turned in different ways, she wondered whether this was true to nature or whether it was by their own will. She would immediately remember her strange relationship with Nagaraja. Sometimes, the thought that maybe Nagaraja was also facing a similar dilemma plagued her. She didn't think it was right to blame Nagaraja completely for her situation because she believed that he, too, had his own wishes, just like her. Just as she found nothing wrong in the park being a part of her, just like he was, she wondered what might have been the root cause for a change in his feelings. The strong suspicion on whether he was craving for some other interest or lifestyle gradually takes on a figure with eyes, nose, face and body. As a result, a part of her became empty. Her lips turned into a regretful smile.

Despite the complexity of whether she could accept Nagaraja completely as she had earlier, the answer was a big zero. Nagaraja, too, must be melting with the same issue. Although she had loved Nagaraja, he was a separate individual. What could she say about him with certainty? No matter what viewpoint was used to look at their relationship, the biggest question was that, lately, the park had come to the forefront beyond everything else. Nagaraja and the park, herself and the park – she was in this inner circle. As she walked in the park with these thoughts in mind, the flowers sang

The Park

softly, and their fragrance soothed her. Also, the chirping of the birds on those trees cheered her up.

That morning, Sumathi woke up as usual. She heard the sounds of some vehicles outside. She just could not believe her eyes as she peeped out of the window. She could hear two to three JCB machines and a few people talking loudly. She felt lost as these sounds entered her ears. The JCB machines were throwing the plants aside. The rows of flowering plants that looked like nursery children wearing colourful clothes were being pulled out with their roots, surrounded by their shrill cries and laments. The flowering creepers looked with totally lost eyes and stood there as orphans, without anyone caring for them. Even the surrounding air was unable to open its mouth. She thought that she could have woken up Nagaraja if he had been there. But lately, he had stopped coming home.

Sumathi came running down. The JCBs continued with their work. As they dug into the soil, picked it up, and threw it to the side, she felt as if her own roots were getting dug up and thrown away. The screams of the flowers-plants-creepers and trees pierced into her and threw her feelings away entirely. She felt like her present state of mind was completely rooted out. As though she had lost everything, she stood there looking at the sky. Moments passed wordlessly. Then, the gentle rays from the faraway Sun entered her eyes and spread all over her body. Glittering light at the edge of the wings of the birds flying in that silvery light. Even from the pain from deep down, a new tune could be heard. The petals of the flowers, too, seemed determined that they would not easily curl up. The emanating tunes mingled with one another, eager to reach another place.

She just stood. A glimmer of hope in her eyes. Her eyelashes were lined with the buds of a garden.

The Turn

Gurumurthy did not have an innate sense of time. At the beginning, he forced himself. The rest of the family did not have any stress or obligations in the morning. On waking up, they tried to loosen their heavy nerves and other parts of the body in a relaxed way, but Gurumurthy realized that his needs were different. The air that moved slowly all around the house suddenly gained speed on reaching Gurumurthy. He had maintained his body to suit this routine. Other than the few words that had to be exchanged in the morning, everything else was moving at a fixed pace like a record player. He knew that only his own mind had to be sharper and faster than all this, and every morning, when he stepped out, the alert Maruti van always supported him as he turned the key in the ignition. As long as that happened, he got the green signal to work.

Gurumurthy enjoyed the caress of the seasonal cool winds against his face. Once he started, the directions, roads, and the houses where he had to stop and pick up the children were all fixed.

Usually, the parents would be waiting at the gate with their children. He was thrilled by the children's lively gait and their delicate words 'Uncle', 'Uncle'. Half his work was done once he dropped them at school. Gurumurthy deliberately helped the children get out of the van. He felt relieved once they safely entered the school campus. Then he chatted for a bit with others who ferried children to school, just like him – Veerabhadra, Vikas, Purushothama, Ningappa and others. He also took up some extra work if time permitted. At school closing time, he returned to drop the children off at their houses, and that concluded his work for the day.

Gurumurthy's father, Ramakrishna, repaired electric appliances. When he had asked his son to learn the customary trade from him, Gurumurthy did not show interest. Ramakrishna was very angry with his son for not studying further after PUC. Although his father used to talk ill about him with others, Gurumurthy felt differently when he saw his mother's expressions. He knew that his father had genuine contempt towards him.

He faced different issues as a student. At night he found his lessons very easy, and every ten minutes, he would say, "Very, very easy… damn easy," loud enough for not only his family but for all the neighbours to hear. "But everything disappears by morning… what to do, *Amma*?" he would lament to his mother, Janakamma. She would say, "Let it go. Everyone can't be smart… somehow you'll find a way. So what if he shouts?" and supported Gurumurthy. Amidst all this, she sometimes worried that this young boy might hurt himself for this reason. 'What do these men know?' she thought and protected Gurumurthy even more. But now she had put a full stop to this.

They only had one daughter, Supriya. She was, by nature, very smart. She was capable of studying for just a quarter of the time the others did and yet scored good marks. Although Gurumurthy hadn't pursued his studies, he wished that his sister Supriya would study at any cost. "You study as much as you want… I will bear the expenses," he had assured her. For this purpose, he invested in a chit fund. But Ramakrishna had something else in mind. In any case, she will complete her degree without any hitch. His stance was to get her married to someone suitable to their family or someone that she likes and finish his responsibilities.

Supriya's world was very different. Gurumurthy knew that it was floating above the ground. He would teasingly call her '*Ammavre*' (madam). This apart, he had great respect for her. He knew that she had big goals. Sometimes, she would say, "Enough. How many more days will you remain single? Get married soon…" Although he did not reply, he felt a sudden bolt of lightning in his body, and a flash of colours rushed to the corner of his eyes. Yet, he said, "Why should I get tied up already?" In order to postpone the talk about his wedding, he talked about how some of his friends who were like mercury earlier had turned mushy, and he laughed.

That day, as the sky was moving from sunset to sunrise, Gurumurthy went to have a cup of tea from the roadside vendor after dropping the children off at school. Veerabhadra, too, had gone there. "What? What had happened? When?" he was talking hurriedly on the mobile phone. He was listening to the reply to his questions with a concerned look. After his conversation, Veerabhadra came closer to Gurumurthy and said, "There's been a problem, *guru* (friend). One of my relatives died at the hospital. They had been trying to contact me since then, but I was not available. Now, they don't have an ambulance to transport his body. My vehicle is *kharaabu* (in bad condition). I'm asking you as a *dost* (friend). Can you help a bit?" Gurumurthy was confused. He had never done such a job before. He thought that it was awkward and remained quiet for some time. By then, Veerabhadra got another call. They must have said something- he approached Gurumurthy, held his hand and said, "This is a very noble work; please don't say no…" Gurumurthy felt as if Veerabhadra's hand had grown twice the size, and his expression was full of frustration because of what had happened in the past few minutes. He also felt a kind of vacuum created within himself. Then he calmed himself down and said, "Okay, give me the details."

After dropping all the children back home, it wasn't difficult for Gurumurthy to reach the location given by Veerabhadra. But there was still some turmoil in his mind. Only after he met the concerned people did it calm down. Their expression of grief, the environment, and the distorted face of the departed painted a different picture. He pulled himself together and prepared himself for further course of action. He rearranged a few things inside the van without making too many changes and got it ready.

The next set of steps was not as emotional. On reaching their house from the hospital, they removed the dead body from the van and placed it in the spot that was already prepared in front of the house. By then, the people at home were informed, and the initial surge of emotions plateaued. They completed the rites as per their custom, and then many men and women touched the departed's hands and feet and paid their respects; they adorned the body with a garland of flowers. Gurumurthy was seriously watching all this. Then, when they asked him to help take it to the graveyard, he agreed with hesitation. In an attempt to adapt to this sudden circumstance, he seemed to have hidden within himself. The dead man was lying inside the van. Those who could not go along were walking about in a frenzy, trying to see and touch the dead body for the last time. Somehow, Gurumurthy felt like the moments were being cut with a saw. Later, they reached the graveyard, and Veerabhadra came on his bike after some time and said 'Thanks' to Gurumurthy. There was no need to tell him explicitly that his job was done. But having been there for so long, he decided to stay till the end. Gurumurthy filled his eyes with all the happenings there. He wasn't so bothered by the surrounding filth. After placing the body on the ground, some last rites were performed. Until then, the surrounding environment felt constricted. After all the formalities were done, the people repeatedly said, 'Thanks', 'it was very helpful' and so on.

After dropping them back to their place and on his drive back home, Gurumurthy felt that the same roads and shops on the way looked new. Only then did he feel happy to have helped some strangers. Also, a few strange strands of emotions were formed. Before blinking, he saw life, which ignited many emotions and expressions; after blinking, he saw death, which brought about aloofness, stillness and an end to everything. Gurumurthy wondered if it was possible to find the exact line between these two; he shook his head, unable to come up with an answer. What a big difference between the excitement and all other behaviours of the children in the morning and later happenings of the day. He realized that he was not very attentive when he was with the children. He decided to certainly immerse himself in that experience as much as possible from then on. In one, there was scope for change and growth. There were chances of ups and downs. It's true that there was no question of any such opportunities in the other. But what about the plight of all other lives that were attached to it? That was very important, he felt. Although he declined, they had forcibly given him twice the money since he was Veerabhadra's friend. Due to this, he felt a little perturbed that what he had done was definitely not purely for friendship.

He spent the next few days picking and dropping the children as usual; the emotions that had surfaced that day had gradually vanished. Just within a week, Gurumurthy got a call again for a similar job. He did not reply immediately. He allowed all his thoughts to flow freely. He was quiet for a few seconds and thought calmly. True, he was earning a fixed income from his regular job. But he had the necessity to go beyond that. It's also true that he was driving some others to their destinations during his spare time. But that was purely business. He figured that, in that case, why not take this up as a business as well? The expenses due to his mother's high diabetes and increasing demands from Supriya also persuaded him to agree to this. When Veerabhadra heard of this, he said, "This is a plus. But first, you must get me sweets, savouries, and coffee. You know why…"

The second time undertaking such a job did not put him through the emotional turmoil it had the first time. He was well aware that he had gone with the family members of the deceased. He did not have much opportunity to mingle with them. He couldn't help watching their actions and the main proceedings. He certainly became quite serious at such times. He also observed people's display of love and respect to the deceased by praying with folded hands, crying, hugging and so on, at their house as well as in the crematorium. Those images stayed in his mind. He did not try to forget them. However, the impact of this showed up in two ways. Word spread that Gurumurthy was available for such jobs, and there was an increased demand for his services.

When the parents of the children whom he ferried to school heard about this, they said, "I believe you transport dead bodies in your free time. Is that so?" He had nodded. "Oh. Is that so? Then we will look for an alternate transport for our *puttu* (little one)," they said. In the beginning, when some of them asked him, he felt somewhat uneasy. But then he began to take a stance, 'So what? What's the big deal? They can stop my services if they want.' Within a month or two, he was completely free from ferrying children in his van and was exclusively using it for dead bodies.

The change in Gurumurthy's routine changed the way his time was divided during the day. But nobody thought it was special. His family were concerned about his phone calls, talks and behaviour. However, since there was no change in his interaction with the family or in his monetary contribution, they did not take it to heart. Only when one of Ramakrishna's customers died did his family know about his job. They seemed to have found the answer to the question that had bothered them lately.

"What is this? We thought that you had an ambulance to ferry patients who were suffering from various diseases or were helpless and weak to the hospital. But what is this, graveyard shift, that you are doing?" yelled Ramakrishna, fuming, as soon as he stepped into their home and narrated all that had happened. Gurumurthy sat silently. All the doubts that Janakamma had were clarified.

She sat boiling in anger. Then she had just retorted, "You have let us down."

Gurumurthy sat without a word. But then he couldn't hold back. "Yes, what's wrong with that? During our great grandfather's times, people stayed far away from death, the dead and their family. They would only dance for birth. I want to know why not for death. That is also equally important, right?" he said in a single breath and walked out. Supriya, who just walked in, pulled him back inside, saying, "Come inside. Let us talk calmly and see." On hearing the news, she sat quietly for some time. Then Janakamma said, "This is all fine, but none of our own issues are settled yet. If you say this now, then what next? Think about it." But knowing fully well that it is meaningless to just talk about it, they simply sat on their own, in deep thought, oblivious of the passing time.

As if to prove Janakamma right, a few families who had approached them with an alliance for Gurumurthy and were preparing to move forward thought to themselves, 'What is this, such a job?' And then they gave some other excuse to Janakamma and called it off. Ramakrishna appeared to be nonchalant and said without turning towards him, "All these days was one kind of *avatara* (awkward), this is another kind of *mahavatara* (more awkward). When was he ever like the others?"

In the circle of van drivers, about five to six of their names ended with 'Murthy'. Out of that, unlike Gurumurthy, some of them were unable to ferry children to school due to their family conditions, economic position, time crunch, and other reasons. Due to this, he was identified and called as 'Children's Murthy'.

Of late, due to the nature of his work, he was called 'Dead body Murthy'. Not only that, some of them hesitated to keep in touch with him out of fear that his job would stick with them or because they lacked the energy to take up the job and for other reasons.

Initially, Gurumurthy felt uneasy while touching the dead body. But now he could easily place the body properly inside the van and take it to the place where it was to be buried or cremated. But the surroundings of the graveyard and crematorium were unspeakably dirty. The entire area seemed to have nothing to do with people and lives. He felt disgusting just to see and breathe. Several dogs and pigs were roaming around happily, eating whatever they found. There was no one to shoo them away. The people who went there were just waiting to finish their work and head back. They only tolerated that environment since they did not have a choice. Those who worked in that office did not step out of the framework of their work. They had adjusted to that dirty environment. All this, which had caused him anguish in the beginning, seemed quite ordinary with time. 'People need this place, don't they?' he wondered. He knew that nothing would get resolved just by feeling disgusted. He felt that it would be nicer if these areas could be kept somewhat clean and had also spoken to the concerned people. But all their assurances turned out to be lies.

Supriya totally disliked Ramakrishna's plans for her future. Her aspirations were not very ordinary. She had resolved to put everything she could at stake to achieve her goals. She just did not agree with her father's idea of sitting quietly and cowering in a corner. She had reined in her conversations with him beyond what was absolutely necessary. She did not trust Janakamma much. She knew about the inhibitions in her mind. As a result, she admired and was proud of Gurumurthy, who followed his own path and manifested his own lifestyle the way he wanted despite everyone condemning him; she was also a bit scared. But no matter what, she believed that he would not abandon her. The recent developments had resulted in her not talking to him as much, but he would talk to her as if nothing had changed. Just like before, he would say, "Madam, this month's chit fund has been paid." She would reply in a slightly excited but clipped manner, "Keep it up." For which he would say, "Is that all… Are your words precious pearls?" and made her laugh.

As Gurumurthy observed more and more dead people's faces, he felt a strange closeness with them. He was so fascinated by the different types of faces of the dead. Some had faces turned towards the right or left, wrinkled faces, chins with a cleft, buck teethed, toothless, with completely closed eyes; a few would have been closed. When he compared his old job and his current job, he felt that the old one had lively children, and the current one had lifeless children. The dead made him wonder about their death - was it quiet, painful, or peaceful, or gone through sorrow or torture? Most of the relatives were in a somewhat anxious state that day, to finish the main thing and get away. They would usually talk about the futility of life or very often go a step further and give him a lecture on happiness in death. Days later, when he contacted them out of curiosity, they would usually sound evasive.

With the onset of Corona, the entire environment began to change. This virus began to infect babies and people of all ages; only apprehension prevailed everywhere. Uncertain about how it would take shape, there was a lot of confusion everywhere. Out of compulsion, the lifestyle of people had changed. This affected all areas of life. People had to follow some important steps to stop the spread, such as social distancing, wearing masks and so on; it became critical for people to stay indoors as much as possible. People took it to the extreme of saying "No… No…", "Maintain distance…" even to talk to each other, shake hands or cuddle anyone else's child, even if they were neighbours or known people. Since this applied to people of all strata, nobody could solve the problems faced, especially by the lower middle class and daily wage workers. The immigrant workers and their families in the state and different parts of the country had taken a beating and were left shaken.

Since the virus spread everywhere much faster than anticipated, a lockdown had to be implemented; despite this, Corona continued to transmit. Infection, test, quarantine, and treatment had to happen one after the other with an uncontrollable intensity. The problems faced due to these were both unexpected and undesirable. As a result, there were throngs of people in the hospitals and nursing homes. Distress and helplessness spread everywhere. A state of uncertainty prevailed, not knowing what would happen to whom at any point in time.

In all this, there was an increase in the number of failed treatments, resulting in the deaths of people infected by Corona. Due to this, a layer of all kinds of fears spread across the nursing homes. Anxious lines filled the eyes of all the people there, especially those who were undergoing treatment, hanging by a thread between life and death. Every time the duty doctors walked by, a flood rose in the hearts of the patient's caregivers, fear of what they might hear next. This made it difficult to find out who, at the nursing home and other dispensaries, was undergoing treatment or whether they were related to a deceased person. If a person had died at the hospital, the air surrounding the deceased sat there kneeling, watching them unblinkingly, with constricted throat, remaining quiet; only when the surrounding air went along with those who went out did it see its own footprint.

Gurumurthy was aware of the overall situation around him, and he handled the death quite well. But he had to deal with those who had died due to Corona quite differently. The relatives had to follow many protocols to get the body released from the hospital to take the next steps. This itself brought in a lot of confusion. The rules were changing on a week-to-week and day-to-day basis. Those who suspected that they were infected, and those who were infected, had to go through all the different Corona-induced stages. The authorities who issued the rules behaved like dictators and imposed severe rules, leaving the relatives feeling very confused. The private hospitals were looting the patients who were infected, whereas the government hospitals were full of deception, and many people were absent from work. But those who were working diligently were overburdened with work. All this information had pervaded Gurumurthy's body and mind.

A person whom he had come in contact with due to his job had died at the hospital from the virus, and Gurumurthy had to attend to further formalities. Veerabhadra was well-connected and knew many people in the circle of authorities. "Look, someone is really bothering me… The person is dead anyway. Why are they causing trouble? Can you please come here?" said Gurumurthy. The person on the other end replied, "It's not such a big deal… I will come there in ten minutes." But when he didn't show up for over two hours, he had to let go of his hope.

When Gurumurthy returned home that day, he was exhausted. Janakamma said, "Somehow, you are looking dull… Sleep if you are tired." He said, "Not at all." But by evening, his body felt a bit hot. He had begun to cough. Supriya, who returned from college, urged him to get tested immediately for any signs of infection. She informed this to Ramakrishna and asked him to join them at the hospital. Gurumurthy felt that Veerabhadra was the right person to suggest to the hospital where he could get an immediate test done, so he asked Supriya to call him. Even after she informed him about the situation, there was a doubt whether Veerabhadra would come. But soon, Veerabhadra came and helped with everything. Ramakrishna, Janakamma and Supriya's only job at the hospital was to sit and wait and nothing more. As soon as they got to know that there were no primary symptoms of the infection, they breathed a sigh of relief. As soon as the family thanked Veerabhadra for taking up all the responsibility, he just cut them off. Only Janakamma, who was silent, had tear-filled eyes.

Gurumurthy was very upset with all the preparation that had to be done before following all the protocols and performing the last rites for the dead. Nobody could touch the body and express their grief. Respectfully paying obeisance, putting a garland as a mark of love or touching the forehead or hands was no longer possible. They could only see the body from afar, suppressing their emotions and remaining stiff. Some of them had an emotional breakdown and collapsed right there because of this restraining rule. And the others there were worried about the condition of the one who had collapsed. It took a lot of time for all this to reach some state of composure. Nobody wanted anything at all, much less talk. They just communicated with hand gestures to finish and leave. Gurumurthy felt that, with Veerabhadra's help, some time and agony could be spared, so he called him again. This time, Veerabhadra spoke much less; he said that he had to drop the children to school and escape. But after that, Gurumurthy felt less troubled by such jobs. As a result, many people realized that he had strong nerves and that he was in great demand.

Ramakrishna stayed home that day due to the lockdown. A man who was around the same age as himself came home in search of Gurumurthy. He said, "I came by to thank Gurumurthy. Look, my friend's son, very young, died of Corona the day before yesterday. The family was depressed that such a thing happened and were clueless. Don't know what would have happened if your Gurumurthy had not taken so much interest and taken care of everything…" Just then, Gurumurthy entered. "Thanks to you. You have done good work," he said. After he left, Ramakrishna looked at Gurumurthy with respect. "All that you're doing… that's enough," he said. Janakamma, who overheard everything, was very happy. "At least you are helping people during difficult times. You are doing a good job," she said.

Within a week or two, the number of deaths increased even more. Although middle-aged and elderly people constituted the majority of these cases, there were also infants who were only a few months old. The lament of those young parents knew no bounds. Not everyone who was infected got hospital care and medicines. Those who did not get it were just collapsing and dying on the streets, footpaths, and just about anywhere. Since no proper arrangements had been made to move the bodies, push carts were also used. People had to stand in long queues at the graveyards and crematoriums just to perform the last rites. There were vehicles with dead bodies on one side, and those who brought them sat next to it. There were vehicles with dead bodies on one side; the one who brought it sat tight next to it. Some of them cursed the entire arrangement. People's minds were filled with strands of anxiety, agitation and rage. Although authorities were holding meetings with experts who gave suggestions on how to curb the spread, there was no improvement. The number of infected and the number of deaths kept increasing day by day. There was no clarity on where things were going wrong. Anybody could say that one of the primary reasons was that the citizens were not following all the protocols to prevent the spread of the virus. Due to this extreme situation, the family did not know when Gurumurthy would come home. They would only watch the deaths and painful happenings in the city on TV.

It was days after the lockdown was lifted. But there was no sign of a decrease in the fatalities. A pall of gloom hung everywhere, like the thick clouds that bring about intermittent rain and veil the sunlight. As soon as he woke up in the morning, Gurumurthy felt like he was hit by an eclipse. That day, it was still semi-dark when he stepped out with an eagerness that had become a rarity in the recent past. People at home only saw him drink the coffee that Janakamma gave him before he left home. His van was like a cute and obedient kid. He glanced at his watch, once holding the steering wheel, and took it to the road. He returned home only at the time when deafening silence descended on the entire city. In between these times, he went from hospital to hospital and from house to house without feeling even a bit weary, as if he wore blinkers on his eyes. Every time, the route would end at the graveyard or the crematorium. All day, it was just the face, hands, legs and eyes of the relatives of the person who died. Unable to touch the body, sad at not being able to see them one last time, many had collapsed in agony, many did not care for the tears dropping from their eyes and tormented themselves, many silently put their heads down and sat all this stuck to Gurumurthy's face and body. Those who used the PPE kit and performed the last rites were in a much better state. At least they could touch the body wrapped in a plastic sheet. Evening, when he was washing his hands at a hotel, he couldn't bear to look at his own reflection and turned his face away. It felt as if people with him were talking from inside a cave. He had just walked out without touching anything. When he reached home that night, Supriya opened the door and was shocked to see him. He did not eat anything but drank two glasses of water and retreated to his room.

That day, Veerabhadra went to Gurumurthy's house to look for him. He met Supriya at the entrance.

"Is Guru home? I came to talk to him."

She said, "Don't you know, the days when he would be home at this time are long gone. What's the matter?" she asked.

"I think you might know... He has made a record."

"Record? What are you saying?"

"So far, nobody has taken as many dead bodies for cremation in a day... He has set that record."

"Is that so? He didn't even tell us." She thought of how Gurumurthy had looked one night in the previous week.

"Ask him to call me when he comes home for lunch."

"Coming home for lunch? We just can't say if he will wonder if he himself knows when he will come home."

"Has it gone so far? You must probably know the reason. People need him; he needs people, that's all."

By then, Janakamma appeared.

She said, "Have you brought your friend with you?"

Supriya told her the news instead of Veerabhadra.

"Oh, has he done all that? That's okay. But who will take care of his whereabouts?"

Supriya looked at Veerabhadra, curious to hear his response. Just then, Veerabhadra's phone rang. As he spoke, "I'm near your house. . . Oh. Okay. I will do that," and then turned to Supriya and said, "He's asking me to go there…" and turned to leave.

"Wait a minute," said Janakamma and went inside. She returned quickly and said, "Look, there are idlis in this… both of you share it." She gave him a packet. He smiled, took it and left.

The Arrival

The next day was Balaji's birthday. Wherever he was, whether he called up or not, his mother Sarasu was sure that he would arrive, as he did every year. How old was he? There was no need to keep count of it. What was needed was a job that he liked and gave him the money he desired, a wife who would tie him down to a place, fulfil all his likings and pacify him. All that Sarasu could do about these two things was just heave a sigh. Let alone others knew about him; she was in a whirlpool of ignorance about him. Finding a bride and conducting the marriage could be taken care of. If he found a job in this place, she would have company. Also, she can take care of him. Whenever she told him all these, his reply was a nought. He would be lost in something else. She felt her tongue dry up, telling him time and again. Finding no other recourse, she got Nagendra, the youngest son of her younger sister, admitted to an undergraduate course at a college nearby. Now, she had someone to talk to in her home. Nagendra was an agile boy. He jelled well with Sarasu. When Balaji's room was vacated for Nagendra to occupy, Nagendra felt as if it was a feast for his eyes. He cleaned the attic and the cupboard. He kept a suitcase that he found in the attic leaning against the wall in a corner.

When Nagendra was selected for the college badminton team, Sarasu remembered the time she had been a member of the kho kho team during her college days. She appreciated Nagendra's interest in sports. She felt that sports kept the body healthy and, along with fulfilling the needs of the body, gave a fillip to cheerfulness; it was also her conviction. Now and then, she used to enquire Nagendra about his participation in sports. Once, she found some free time somehow to coincide with his playing hours and watched him play. In addition, the *chow chow bath*, a sweet snack she had prepared for all the boys, delighted them. But Balaji had steered clear of all these when he studied in school and college. Though Sarasu tried a few times to persuade him to take up sports, she gave up, concluding that he was not interested in it. Besides, her husband Ramachandra told her strictly to allow Balaji to be himself. In all, Balaji had complete freedom, and he danced in joy. Sarasu had no clue about Balaji's studies, movements, friends or hobbies, and she was perplexed. If she had an inkling of it, there was room for questions. It was absent, and everything was a void. She rode on just assumptions.

When Balaji completed his undergraduate course, securing first-class marks, Sarasu was happier than Balaji felt about his own achievement. She felt as if a veil of darkness was lifted from her eyes, and colourful lights streamed in. While he was at home, Balaji was as good as a dumb person, and so was an enigma. Is it possible to comprehend the behaviour of the waves of the mind of a boy growing up? Sarasu and Ramachandra believed that the more a youngster's mind is let free, the more it gains lustre, gets an opportunity to mingle and be grafted, and forms a layer of ambitions of becoming strong. Accordingly, he came out with flying colours even in his post-graduate course. Sarasu and her husband had no place in his thoughts about what he wished to do next. As always, he kept to himself, and knowing his ways of acting completely according to his wish, they did not venture to probe further. Besides, right from the beginning, Balaji had the determination to get what he wanted. The parents did not even know ten percent of his routine, movements, friends, interests or hobbies. In all, they knew very little of the world he had created for himself. Sometimes, they felt that his peers might know more about him, but no suitable chance came by to test it. When opportunities did crop up, they were not used properly. Later, they regretted it.

Mysurupak was Balaji's favourite sweet, right from his childhood. He not only savoured it after it was prepared, brightening his face but also observed carefully every stage of its preparation. In the end, Sarasu poured the thick syrup onto a plate and cut it into squares. The knife she used for doing so did not digress even a little and moved straight as if it were drawn with a scale. Many times, Balaji had watched this and clapped in joy. Since he had a special liking for the sweet, Sarasu was very much interested in offering it to him, if not on other days, at least on his birthday. That apart, the joy she felt when he fared well in his undergraduate and post-graduate examinations was such that she prepared it for all his friends.

Now, she remembered Balaji's fondness for *Mysurupak* well in advance, and before it was evening, she went to Parimala Stores located near the bus stand and bought half a kilogram of the sweet. She had finished the task apprehensive that there would be no streetlights at night due to long hours of power outage in summer. Besides, Nagendra had informed her that he would return home late after participating in the function organised to commemorate his team's victory in the tournament.

Sarasu lighted the gas stove, set the cooker to boil rice, and sat on the chair for a few minutes. She was worried that her family was unlike that of others. A major turning point in her life was the death of Ramachandra. He had occupied quite a top post in a prestigious company. He died after suffering a heart attack when he was in his office. Sarasu secured a job on compassionate grounds according to her overall eligibility, but getting it was not as easy as she had assumed it would be. Though fifteen years had passed by, when she closed her eyes, it appeared as if it happened yesterday. Other than Balaji, Sarasu had a daughter, Bhuvi, who was a replica of Ramachandra. Sarasu derived happiness and elation from Bhuvi when she completed her undergraduate course in biochemistry, securing high marks. Later, Bhuvi flew to America. More than the people and the place, she felt that, from the perspective of career prospects, the environment here was akin to hell. For Sarasu, it was the same story with respect to Bhuvi's marriage. But for giving her blessings, everything else had been organised by Bhuvi. In fact, their relationship was maintained only through the telephone. Bhuvi had not been directly responsible for the present situation in any way. Her expectations were limited to what an ordinary married woman would have. She was about five-and-a-half feet tall and pale brown in complexion. On seeing her from a distance of ten feet, it was very proper for one to feel that she was most ordinary. But, if one came near her, the shine in her eyes compelled one to accord respect to her.

"Ding-dong", the sound of the calling bell brought Sarasu back to her senses.

On opening the door, she saw Sharadamma who lived in the opposite house. She repeated the news about the impending marriage of a relative and said, "I asked Priya to accompany me. She isn't paying heed. She says her examinations are drawing near, and so she won't go … Tomorrow, you attend the wedding along with her".

"Will do so gladly … Let her have her lunch here … I'll call her".

"No … I've cooked for her", said Sharadamma and left with the others.

Just then, the agent who delivered newspaper to Sarasu's house turned up. He held the last month's bill before her.

"Your boys don't deliver the newspaper regularly … After I notice that it hasn't been delivered and call you up, you send it to me", said Sarasu with impatience.

"When the permanent staff don't turn up, I've to send the new boys … I do tell them … But, they forget …", he grinned.

"If it keeps recurring, I'll subscribe from a different vendor".

"It won't happen again", he said.

Priya used to burn the midnight oil studying, unlike Nagendra. Almost every night, Sarasu woke up once to go to rest room, and when she glanced, she would notice Priya studying even at half past one o'clock. Sarasu admired Priya's hard work. She wished that if this girl were a little older, she could be married to Balaji; she smiled at her foolish wish. Besides, she justified herself by thinking that it was normal for everybody to wish for the best, whatever the circumstance they were living in.

By force of habit, Sarasu switched on the television. She felt bored watching the clichéd scenes, and just as she switched it off, Revappa arrived. In the mornings, Revappa used to deliver packets of milk and curd after collecting coupons for them. He said, "You'd asked me to look for a bride for your son. I've in mind a girl hailing from our village. It's actually my native place. I don't know the sub-caste to which she belongs. She's just completed matriculation. Everything else is excellent". Sarasu responded: "That doesn't matter. The boy and the girl should like each other", and turned her back to him. Revappa drawled: "By the way, it's been quite a long time since you came to stay in this house. Your son doesn't seem to have come here even once".

"Well, he may arrive tomorrow. I'll inform you". Sarasu felt what he said was true. These three years had passeby quickly without anybody noticing Balaji's arrival and departure.

"Please do so … If the girl becomes part of your family … It'd be the best thing to happen … As good as gold". As she recalled these words of Revappa, new hopes and expectations arose in her.

Nagendra came home a little while after there was a power outage. He told Sarasu that dinner had been arranged by the college authorities. When he entered his room in the dim light, he tripped over the suitcase that he had kept leaning against a wall. It opened up.

After having dinner, Sarasu finished her chores. She sat down for some time and skimmed through the newspaper of the day.

Before she went to bed, she noticed that there was light in Priya's room.

It must've been past midnight. Sarasu did not find any relief from thoughts crowding her mind. She was only half asleep, just tossing and turning in bed. There was no noise of traffic on the road. Now and then, a dog barked. The burden of silence used to frighten her frequently. But she had gotten used to it and neglected it. Some sounds that seemed to tear apart the silence that had spread around did not appear to be of any significance. But, suddenly, she heard someone screaming intermittently. She felt that the voice was that of Priya's and woke up. When it did not increase and continue to be heard, she thought that she must have imagined it. Now, she heard more of the screaming, and there was no room for doubt. It was indeed Priya's

Sarasu woke up with a start. When she opened the door and moved in the dim light, Priya's feeble voice started getting closer. Though there was nobody on the road, she stumbled. When she was back on her feet, her hand picked up a stick lying nearby. Holding the stick in her hand, she peeped through the window of Priya's room.

What she saw made her shriek, "Priya ..." She noticed that Priya's dress was tattered. A man had covered her mouth, preventing her from screaming. He tried to rape her. Priya's hands were moving around. In a moment, Sarasu was at her doorstep. When she shouted again, "Priya", the man inside must have become aware of the changed circumstances. He pushed Priya aside. Sarasu's attention was focused on Priya. Priya was unable to speak. The attacker tried to push Sarasu, who had blocked the doorway and tried to escape. Sarasu did not give him any chance to do so, shouting, "Scoundrel," and striking him on his head with the stick. She could only notice that he fell down. She barely saw him fall before she collapsed.

After Sarasu recovered from the shock dealt by the incident and returned to normalcy, she opened her eyes and realised that she had been made to lie down in her house. Nagendra, with a serious bearing, was sitting at a distance. He came near her and touched her hand. He addressed her: "Aunty". Seethamma, Sarasu's neighbour, made her sit up. Another lady gave her a glass of water.

There was faint light outside. Sarasu thought that the night had passed. Though she did not know the reason for her plight, when the details of the incident began to pass before her eyes as if they were projected on a screen, she began sobbing. She asked those next to her, "How is Priya keeping?" Seethamma conveyed to her what the doctor had said after the preliminary examination: "Nothing untoward has happened to her". As Sarasu let out a sigh of relief, waves of joy arose in her mind and gave liveliness to her body. As if hinting at her curiosity to know details of other matters, she asked, "What about the wretched fellow?"

"He has got his due".

"Meaning?"

Seethamma reported that as soon as Sarasu shouted, a few men from the houses in the vicinity came running one after the other and, upon learning of the sensitivity of the situation, took appropriate action. Since the attempt to rape was a very grave issue, the police arrived soon. They took some photographs and wrote down something. They shifted Priya to a hospital and took the man away in the condition he was found in. Meanwhile, the address of the place of the wedding to which Sharadamma had gone was gathered, and she was brought back. As this was being said, Saharadamma came in, crying, "Sarasu, you saved my daughter. You are her real mother". Unable to say anything further, she hugged Sarasu.

As the morning passed and the routine of the people went on, the news spread very fast on the road on which Sarasu lived, as well as the roads in front of and behind it. People of different ages began dropping in to enquire, leading one to fear that it might obstruct the movement of vehicles. Those who came let loose their guesses and imaginations along with the abundant details they had gathered from the relatives of Sarasu and Sharadamma. Be that as it may, Sarasu became a superwoman in the eyes of all. Besides, Priya was deemed a lucky girl. Listening to people hail her, "Superwoman! Superwoman!" Sarasu felt pleased with herself and gave a gentle smile to those who said so.

In the backdrop of people coming to Sarasu and praising her, she thought, initially, that anybody would have done the same, and there was nothing extraordinary about it. Gradually, she began to feel that her act was not an ordinary one. The feeling that she was a superwoman, as was being attributed by all, took deeper roots, and her ears and eyes became sensitive. She felt pleased about it, and her expectation that people should call her so increased. Earlier, she used to speak very sparingly because she was a little shy. Increasingly, she started speaking more.

All of a sudden, she remembered that it was the day Balaji was supposed to arrive. She beckoned to Nagendra, who was somewhere over there, and, in a whisper, asked him to keep *Mysurupak* packet safe.

A woman from next door drew near. She poured coffee into a tumbler and handed it to Sarasu. "Don't get into the business of cooking for today. Take rest. That's it. I've informed Sharadamma too", she said and caressed Sarasu's shoulder. When Sarasu told her, "Why do you take the trouble?" the woman paid no heed. The visitors responded to Sarasu in ways they could think of: talk, touch or sight. Afterwards, they realised that their job was done, and spending time there doing nothing became burdensome. Sarasu, too, realised the difficulty they faced, and as she turned away from them, they nodded or waved their hands and left, one by one.

When only Nagendra and she were left behind in the house, Sarasu cursed herself for not having looked up Priya.

"I'll call on Priya", she said and got up. She noticed that a little blood had come out of the wound on her right heel. Ignoring it, she went to Priya's house and stood at the doorway. She received a special welcome. Sharadamma approached her, taking long strides, and, extending her hand, invited Sarasu: "Come in … Come in …" Sarasu found the welcome unusual, a little unnatural, and felt embarrassed. She hesitated to feel at home. However, she did not make it known. She went to the place where Priya was lying down and sat before her. She did not know what to say. "Bad times … But, it passed …" she said, pausing many times. Priya did not see Sarasu in the eye.

After the lapse of some time, she tried to say something to the effect, "Grateful to you …" in a very low voice and kept quiet. Sharadamma stood by.

"Go to sleep", said Sarasu and got up.

She remembered Balaji. Though he would not give his whereabouts or other details, usually, he used to arrive on the morning of his birthday; he would not even call up sometimes. Let alone others, Balaji knew how much happiness he derived from doing so. But why was it so now? Had something untoward? If he had to shoulder the responsibility of a family, everything would have fallen into place. Sarasu thought of calling him to find out, but Balaji had the habit of changing the number on his phone frequently. He should arrive out of his own volition. She thought that she could not do anything else than just wait.

It was only after she returned home that her attention was focused on the wound. When she examined it, she saw that blood was dripping from it. Thinking that neglecting it would invite trouble, she set out to get it dressed. By then, the movement of pedestrians and vehicles on the road had reached the normal level. Those who mounted their vehicles to go to the office, those who set out along with them in a hurry to drop their children to school, handcarts that sold vegetables, and all the others created an environment that was mixed with tension. But, strangely, the news that she was a superwoman had spread in the entire surroundings. Acquaintances and even strangers waved to her, gave a gentle smile, and raised their hands. Some whispered, "Great, aunty!" when they came close to her and moved on. As she hobbled, she felt that all these combined to form a layer of shining gold on the ground. Preoccupied with these thoughts, she felt a little lost, and before she might collide with somebody, she thought of removing them from her mind. She felt relieved that whatever her own plight, Priya did not suffer greater trouble. Otherwise, what might have happened? How much of a nuisance and commotion would it have produced? How would Priya have faced it, fought back, and turned into a stronger human being? Phew! All that was avoided. With these thoughts running through her mind, she climbed the steps to the hospital nearby. By then, some of the people there had come to know quite a lot of details of the incident. Since Priya had been brought there the last night, everything had been widely discussed.

When Sarasu walked to the OPD, some of the doctors and the nurses who walked past her said, quivering their eyebrows: "You did the right thing". Others said, "Timely work", and expressed their appreciation with a gentle smile. Recalling all that had happened since morning, Sarasu imagined that she was made to sit and people came in a line, one by one, and served her dishes usually prepared during festivals.

When Sarasu said that she wanted to get her wound dressed, two nurses vied with each other to attend to her. As if Sarasu had been struck a major blow, the nurses applied medicine, bandaged it, and caressed it gently. One felt if so much fuss was needed to dress such a small wound. Sarasu felt exhausted as a result of all that had happened one after the other; she wanted to keep all of them away. Now, the pleasant feeling given by the warm Sun early in the morning had disappeared. The heat was increasing slowly.

The Arrival

Sarasu reached home, walking slowly, taking care to avoid pieces of stone and small objects that lay strewn on the road. She did not pay attention to anything that she saw or heard on her way back home.

Nagendra had gone to college. The woman living next door came in to give Sarasu a box with lunch in it, just as she did for members of her family.

The newspaper delivery boy must have come by. Sarasu picked up the newspaper lying in a corner of the front yard and sat on a chair. As usual, by the time she read some of it and folded it up, about three-quarters of an hour had lapsed. She looked up at the clock and thought that, let alone Balaji's arrival, there was not even a phone call from him. Perhaps he must not have been able to find any free time due to hectic work or some other reason. Else, did he not remember it was the day his birthday was being celebrated or the date of his birth at all? The thought that it was plausibly crossed her mind. Whatever the situation, however, be it, let circumstances permit him to come home; the wish started growing all over her being. Since there had been no instance of Balaji not being home on his birthdays, Sarasu felt the same thing would happen this time, too and felt a little relieved.

The evening set in. Nagendra came home. He saw Sarasu's sad face and tried to speak to her. But, he kept quiet and, as usual, went to play.

The night paved the way for morning. Sarasu felt heavy in her body as she did not sleep well. So, she got up late. Though she did not feel like it, the pressure of routine pressed her. She did not want to wake up Nagendra. She crossed the threshold holding the coupons for milk and curds. On the road, a few people she saw kept to themselves as they passed by. When Sarasu held the coupon before Revappa, he bore a grave expression.

"Do you have any news of the girl? When are they going to come?" she asked him.

Revappa did not reply. Every day, he gave the packets of milk and curds immediately. But now, holding another bag up, he took out Balaji's photograph that Sarasu had given him earlier and returned it to her.

When she asked him, "Don't you need it to show it to the girl's family?" he just put the packets of milk and curds into the bag that she had brought with her.

Sarasu could not make out anything. She assumed that something untoward must have happened in the girl's family. The others who came to Revappa's shop to buy milk as late as her did not look at her and left hurriedly after their job was done.

When she came home, she noticed that the newspaper was not lying on the ground in the front yard. She saw the woman living next door. She remembered that she had not returned the lunch box and went to her to give the box that had been washed. The woman took it, and even before Sarasu thanked her, she went in and called out her son's name. Questions cropped up in Sarasu. Finally, she thought that something was unusual in their house.

"Wretched fellow! Don't know where he is. It's fine if he could not make it, but what prevents him from informing me?" She cursed Balaji while she prepared coffee. She woke up Nagendra and gave him coffee. She, too, drank coffee and, wanting to look up Priya, set out of the house.

As soon as she pressed the calling bell, Sharadamma appeared at the door. She glared at Sarasu as if she had seen a ghost and stood stiff.

"Did you come to check whether she is alive or not?"

Sarasu was stunned.

"Why? What happened?" asked Sarasu, feeling as if she had dashed her head against the wall.

"How can I bring myself to say it …? Haven't you come to know yet?"

"What should I come to know?"

Sharadamma turned her face away and asked, "Haven't you read the newspaper?" She picked up the newspaper lying on the teapoy, turned a few pages and held it at Sarasu's face.

Balaji's photograph was published with the title that a serial rapist had been arrested! Sarasu blacked out and collapsed.

When she regained consciousness, she noticed that Nagendra was sitting next to her, and she was in her house. She noticed that the newspaper was lying on the corner of the bed.

Both of them sat in silence for a long time. At one point in time, Sarasu felt as if all the sounds in the surroundings had stopped suddenly. At another, she felt as if all the sounds were amplified a hundred times and assaulted her ears. Her life of all these years and her struggles appeared to be blazing in front of her eyes.

Nagendra noticed that Sarasu shook her body a little and turned to her. He could not muster the courage to speak to her even now. Nothing flashed in his mind, and though he knew all the thinking he did simply would be futile, he sat down doing the same. He waited to see what Sarasu had to say and what she would do. He had foregone attending college that day.

The verandah was fully lit now. Sarasu's face developed a graver expression. In her view, Nagendra was an innocent child. She thought, "What can I tell him? Is it hard to say anything to him?

She felt heavier in her body because she had been sitting in the same place. She got up and went towards the wash basin. Nagendra's eyes followed her. Seeing her face in the mirror, she closed her eyes. She washed her face with her eyes closed and felt scared to open them. After splashing more water on her face, she opened her eyes and swallowed saliva. When she walked back, Balaji's suitcase, which Nagendra had put aside, opened up fully after she hit her leg on it. Seeing its contents, Sarasu leaned against the wall and lifted her neck. The suitcase contained bras and panties. Nagendra looked at Sarasu and the contents of the suitcase. Since Sarasu's back leaning against the wall was sliding down, he held her and made her sit up. Her plight flummoxed him. He was not sure if he had to call the neighbours. Immediately, he fetched a glass of water and placed it in her hand. He gained some courage, seeing that she held it in her hand. He made her bring the glass of water close to her mouth. Sarasu was gazing elsewhere. Nagendra made her see the glass of water. When she drank the water, he gained some more courage.

Just a few minutes must have passed. When Sarasu said, "Get up. Let's go", Nagendra wondered from where she had gained so much energy and looked at her. It appeared to him that she had firmed up more than usual. He could not figure out her purpose.

"Where's the packet of *Mysurupak*?"

Nagendra fetched it.

She opened the cover of the suitcase fully and pushed all its contents inside. She banged the cover, and it closed tight.

Outside the house, the Sun was blazing. The amount of heat that fell on Sarasu's head made her feel as though a pan containing red hot charcoal had been placed on it. All over her body, she felt as if she had worn a dress of fire. The air was pushed aside by vehicles passing by now and then, and it felt like embers thrown at her. The road was deserted. With Sarasu holding the suitcase and Nagendra holding the packet of *Mysurupak*, both of them stood on the road turning their necks around for a while. The doctor, who had raised his eyebrow in appreciation of Sarasu, passed by in his car. He did not even glance at them. Now and then, autorickshaws plied at such a distance that they could not be hailed.

Sarasu had not paid attention to the time. When she observed that their shadows were not visible to them, she realised what time it was. The heat seemed to rend their skin and get inside. Finding it difficult to look around, they just saw each other a couple of times.

Sarasu told Nagendra, "You should've worn your cap". He touched his head and said, "Not a problem".

The hot breeze was blowing. Among the shops seen at a distance, two had downed their shutters by half to ward off the heat of the Sun. The other two had big balloons hanging on one side and slippers swinging to and fro on the other.

"Did you have something to eat?"

Nagendra just looked at her.

After some time passed, Sarasu noticed an autorickshaw, and when it drew near, she hailed it and said, "Police station". The driver of the autorickshaw looked on with a fixed gaze. Though he behaved in a suspicious manner, he agreed to the ride either due to fear or something else.

Both of them did not speak till the autorickshaw travelled some distance. Sarasu could not make out what was passing by that appeared like moving images. Besides, there was a mixture of unclear sounds and silence. As they sat in the autorickshaw, a very hot breeze struck their cheeks and ears. Dust mingled with it and made it difficult for them to open their eyes. Though they wiped their eyes once, they did not feel fine. When Sarasu turned to Nagendra, she saw that he held the packet of *Mysurupa*k in one hand and rubbed his forehead with the other. She felt pity for Nagendra because he had to be a part of such a heightened and tension-ridden situation for no reason. She just kept a hand on the suitcase and another on Nagendra's knee gently.

The Arrival

When Sarasu had travelled on the road many times, she had noticed the board of the police station but not paid attention to anything else around it. It was only now, when she alighted from the autorickshaw, that her eyes fell on them. Within the compound wall of the police station, there were vehicles that were half-bent, lifted up partially, and with one or the other wheel missing. Autorickshaws that looked like skeletons were the prominent ones among the vehicles lying there. All of them were only half alive. It was impossible for them to breathe and become functional again.

In the yard of the police station, there were three groups of people. Women were on one side, and men were on the other. Each group had about four or five people in it. Some of the groups seemed to be burning fiercely and boiling, while the others seemed defeated and lifeless. On noticing Sarasu and Nagendra, they glanced at them for a fraction of a second and turned back, losing themselves in their whispering.

A policeman was standing there, holding a rifle. A little distance away from him, another one sat behind a table with a register. Sarasu told the policeman holding the rifle, "I want to meet the inspector". Without speaking, he pointed his finger towards the table. Sarasu went to him.

She told him, "The day before yesterday night, a man was arrested. I want to meet the inspector".

He lifted his neck up and asked, "Who're you referring to?"

"He's named Balaji". Listening to this, he stared intensely.

"You are …?"

"Sarasu"

On listening to the name, he opened his eyes widely. From where he sat, he looked inside the police station. When Sarasu and Nagendra looked in that direction, they saw the inspector's chamber. They heard some conversations going on.

"Please be seated for a minute, Madam. You can go in as soon as the inspector is free".

Emerging from inside another part of the police station were loud voices of someone shouting and someone wailing. They quietened for a couple of seconds, only to resume soon.

Sarasu looked in. She saw cells that had doors with iron bars. There were men and women inside them. In the middle of the station, she saw another man sitting amidst many registers. On the other side, framed photographs of notorious criminals were hung on the wall.

When the man said, "You can go in now", Sarasu walked in accompanied by Nagendra.

She went into the inspector's chamber.

He lifted his head up. She told him, "I'm Sarasu. The day before yesterday night …"

Interrupting her, he said, "I know. Please sit down. How're you doing?"

She sat down and looked at Nagendra. He, too, sat down in the chair next to hers.

"Bastard ... He's an old hand ... We'd been looking for him a lot ... You've done something really good".

She lowered her head.

"His fate is sealed ... What brings you here?"

"I want to meet him", she said with hesitation.

"Well ... Not a problem ... Anything else?"

She shook her head.

"I'll inform you when you're needed in the court ... Let me know if it's difficult for you to attend. I'll send someone. This boy is?"

"A relative"

The inspector pressed the button under his table. A sound was heard outside.

In a rough voice, he told the person who turned up immediately, "The scoundrel we brought in the day before yesterday ... Take them to him. Hey! Keep an eye on them. Hope you understand".

As they had done when they entered, Sarasu and Nagendra got up, holding the suitcase and the packet in their hands. The policeman noticed it and turned to the inspector.

"Don't bother. Go with them".

The policeman took them to the cell in which Balaji was housed. He was wearing a white shirt and white shorts. He had been leaning against the wall, looking somewhere. Hearing some sound near the door of the cell, he stood up.

Though there was not enough light, he could make out who had come. He turned his face away. He did not budge from where he was standing. Sarasu closed her eyes for a couple of seconds and opened them. He remained the same. She tried to restrain her mixed feelings that were gushing forth, yet her eyes were moistened. She swallowed her saliva without being conscious of it. She had sacrificed all that had belonged to her. Nagendra was new to all these. He could not decide what to do. Without having to put in any effort, many things that he had never seen began filling up in him. Having been stiff in the beginning, he loosened himself up a little. He leaned his hand on one of the bars of the door. Sarasu leaned herself against it.

The constable who accompanied them told Balaji, "Someone has come to meet you … Come here".

As Balaji began walking towards the door, his face could be seen better. He stood close by within arm's reach. He had put his face down.

Sarasu took the packet of *Mysurupak* from Nagendra, opened it, clutched a palmful of it and held it near his face. He did not react.

"Take it", she said quite loudly.

As if he was subjected to a strange kind of compulsion, Balaji came closer. Nagendra and he kept looking on. Sarasu opened Balaji's mouth with her left hand and forced the contents of her fist into it. The next moment, she threw the packet at his face. He lifted his face due to the sudden shock. Sarasu gathered all her strength and went on slapping him. He leaned to a side.

Before the others could realise what she was up to, she opened the suitcase and started throwing fistfuls of its contents at him.

The constable stopped her. Immediately, two policemen came running, snatched the suitcase and took her aside. The inspector heard the commotion and came out of his chamber. He did not feel like talking to her immediately. The constables made her sit down on a bench. And, Nagendra too who was frightened.

The inspector was baffled to see Balaji and the things lying around in the cell. He could not figure out anything for the moment and ordered the things to be tied into a bundle.

He came near Sarasu, who was sitting at a distance and asked her, "What's going on?" She kept quiet. His curiosity egged him on.

He asked her gently, "Did you talk to him?"

She continued to keep quiet.

The inspector turned to Nagendra.

"He is her son".

The inspector looked at Sarasu in disbelief. Sarasu's eyes seemed to look nowhere.

The inspector could not bring himself to say anything. He just pressed both her hands gently and left.

Later, Sarasu and Nagendra sat on a bench in the yard. Some more time passed. A constable threw the pieces of *Mysurupak* outside the compound wall to a distance. Stray dogs moving around carried them in their mouths.

A few seconds later, Nagendra moved aside, bent down, and placed his head on Sarasu's lap. She rested her head against the wall and gently placed her hand on his head.

The Monsoon

Nanjundaiah stood in the compound and gazed at the expanse of the sky. There were only a few grey clouds in the blue; as the evening light entered his eyes, the weight on his thick eyebrows eased a bit. He went to his room and wore a loose shirt and pants as usual. Just as he was stepping out, Rekha called out to him from behind. She said, "Carry the umbrella, *mavayya* (father-in-law)… it's monsoon season, isn't it? Can't say when it'll start raining…" As soon as he stepped back in, she turned and walked away. Nanjundaiah glanced at her, picked up his old umbrella, and left.

His legs habitually took him on that road. The surrounding sights and sounds had the usual shades and nothing special. The movement and sounds of the vehicles on the road reflected their driver's state of mind. He often came across people who walked there just like him. He was only familiar with their faces. He blended in without being perturbed by the movement and action of these people who were engrossed in their own world.

Since his retirement two years ago, he would take a walk every morning and evening for an hour and a half each. Before retirement, one of his colleagues, who was twenty years younger but very outspoken, had asked him, "What, sir… all this convenience, company, power, pride and everything that you're used to, for the past three and half decades; in a way, life in the society... I mean, does it feel like you are just breathing and have lost everything else? When you lose all these, tell me the truth." Looking at his grim face, Nanjundaiah replied, "Look... the truth as I know, is – to retire doesn't mean to lose everything, it means to get... mainly the remaining time... but also note one point: to attain whatever a person holds in his palm is decided by each person's situation, that's all. You know what I mean by situation..." he said, laughing. As soon as he stepped into the park, he saw a brown-skinned, medium build person who more or less looked like him; this incident suddenly came to mind.

Nanjundaiah pondered as he sat. In the past forty-five minutes since he entered the park, this was the second van with a dead body heading towards the electric crematorium. His calculations were usually not wrong since the electric crematorium was at the end of his walking path. He saw some unusual scenes of such vans about two or three times a week. 'If I had a camera, I would have immediately clicked a picture', he thought. He saw snapshots that evoked surprise, sorrow, intense feelings and other emotions in him. But within a few seconds, those emotions disappeared, and he continued to walk unattached. Even amidst all this, a sneer sometimes appeared on his lips. When he saw the decoration on the dead bodies and the behaviour of the accompanying people, which included loud cries and noises, Nanjundaiah was surprised at how death was celebrated, which would put life to shame. He wanted to understand the core and the beginning of this belief. But he realised that it was impossible. 'Is mindset a concrete object or a glimpse of a scene... which can be photographed first in order to learn lessons from it later?' he realised the futility of trying and kept quiet. He also raised his eyebrows in amazement at the limits in all facets of life.

Many times, when he looked at the van transporting the dead body, he felt as if he was one among those sitting around the body or dancing, and his body felt a bit hot. More often, he felt as if he was the dead body in the van and rows of sweat beads formed on his bald head. A couple of times, he picked up the pen and paper and began to pen it all down – he thought it would help to share such unique experiences, not only with other people but also for him to ruminate over and over again. But within one or two sentences, he felt tired and beaten and thought, 'It has almost been half a century since I last wrote an exam like this. I get only double zero marks for my pathetic writing.' He smiled, crumpled the paper and threw it away. He realised his limits. Later, he sipped the coffee that his daughter-in-law Rekha gave him, slower than usual; then, he got up and walked outside with heavy footsteps into the twilight.

Lately, his son Shivaram's nippy, negligent attitude and indifference towards him were increasing; he wondered how his son could be so different from him in character and behaviour. His own son was such a different man. How is it he was completely unable to understand the inner workings of his son? He had wondered countless times and had finally given up, unable to find any reason. Many occasions had irked him immensely. Depending on the intensity of the situation, Rekha realised that disaster might strike if the invisible line was crossed and tried to build bridges between them. But even during such attempts, she invariably had some limitations, and the objective was not met. The first time he faced such heat was a few years back. He had only recently retired. The office had given him most of his dues on the day of retirement itself. He had already given it a lot of thought and decided that in order to make good use of it, he had given it towards the purchase of a site in Shivaram's name. It was like a resolution for Nanjundaiah. "Look, Shivaramu, my father never thought that one needs a house to live in till the last breath. His life was without any desires, just happy with the necessities being met. Haven't you heard of Purandaradasaru - '*allide nanna mane, illi bande summane*' (my house is there, and I simply came here) – that kind? Then, about me, although I had the desire, I didn't have the strength. I spent my days in changing rented houses. You should not go through that plight. I've done whatever I can. It's up to you to build the house," he said, and Shivaram was made happy by this unexpected gesture. Since Shivaram didn't express anything in words, Nanjundaiah assumed that it must have been due to the love and respect he had towards him. Somehow, that day, Shivaram looked like a high school student to him.

It took two months after retirement to get the balance amount. At that time, for some reason, he didn't feel like collecting it himself. It was also probably because he had found a few books that he had been meaning to read for a long time and was engrossed in reading them. His office reminded him three times to collect it, and every time, he asked Shivaram to do it. But every time, Shivaram gave some excuse. Although the first two times he felt it was genuine, the third time it felt suspicious. "What, sir, you seem to be busier now than before. How can everyone be as busy?... please keep it up," said his office colleagues, partly in jest and in appreciation when he finally went to collect the money. Shivaram continued to religiously follow this policy that took birth at that time. He had turned Nanjundaiah's expectations upside down. That is when Nanjundaiah began to cut down his conversations.

He did not have to fear the inevitable feeling of loneliness after retirement. Among the hobbies he had developed since his younger days, the craze for reading was one. He used to joyously enter the alternate universe that it opened for him. He loved to engage himself in it totally. His thoughts about it were different. He went in search of young Raghunath, who was still in service, just to share it with him. Raghunath, who was immersed in a file, laughed softly and said, "I am not free until I finish this audit. Wait, I'll come. I'm almost done. Anyway, this is like your parents' house, right…" True, this used to be the office where he had worked. But how did it look so new?... A different shade even in the familiar faces. Although he had belonged here once, why was he unable to become a part of it now? Was his retirement such a big issue? For some time, he sat looking around like an audience. Amidst all this, someone perhaps called out his name. He felt so. "Goodness, if we stay here, someone or another will keep annoying me. Let's go to the canteen where there won't be any such issues," Raghunath said, leading him to the canteen. Raghunath finished narrating the latest news from the office over a cup of coffee and a cigarette. Nanjundaiah did not react to anything. He stared at the pathway for a few seconds, then he laid the foundation for his subject, "Look Raghu, I feel that the statement, reading and books are best friends, is just nonsense… I'm not saying a word about their greatness, need, uses and other things. I'm only against calling it a friend. Because it provides us with a whole new world – even if you say entirely - it's true. It is possible for me to react to it. But there is no reply to my words. A discussion, unlike a friend, is missing. One-way traffic says, let whatever is yours stay within you. Look, even to share this thought, a friend is needed. What do you say?" He stared and looked at him thoughtfully and gave it some thought with his eyes half closed, and then said, "Truly Nanjundi, what a blow you gave. It is one hundred percent true. Due to all this, not only do I feel more affectionate towards you, but also jealous." Later, when he was about to leave, he laughed and said, "You better not forget that I'm your friend."

Raghunath insisted on taking him to the hotel in the corner; they had spent countless hours thereafter office, engaged in intense discussion on all the worldly matters, as if they had to carry all that burden themselves, losing track of time. As usual, they had coffee with onion, potato and ridge gourd *bajjis* (fritters), and they opened their hearts out and spoke without any restraint. It was seven thirty when they walked out.

The house was locked when he got back. He enquired with the neighbours for the keys, but none of them had it. He sat at the doorstep, waiting. It was summer; he could not keep the mosquitos away even by covering his face with a kerchief. He kept looking left and right for Shivaram-Rekha since he didn't know which direction they would come from and waited quietly. Somehow, he was reminded of the day when he had failed the math exam during his degree course and had sat outside the house for hours, unable to bring himself to knock on the door, even though his parents were home. It was past ten when they returned home. Aravind ran up to him and hugged him. Shivaram was nonchalant. As he unlocked the door, Rekha was flustered and said, "Why were you sitting here, *mavayya*... He forgot to give the key to the neighbour. Why didn't you sit in a friend's house..." He replied, "Who is my friend here... they are just acquaintances... They just say hello if I bump into that too, only if they raise their head and look at me."

As the night began to descend, and the darkness united with light, the feelings that were caused by the images he saw earlier changed into a more soothing one, probably the result of his interest in photography. His keen eyes, which were trained to observe such things, noticed it immediately. The number of people who had come to the park for the evening walk had reduced.

Broken bricks were arranged to make a six-foot-wide walkway; a person walked slowly down that path and then sat on the stone bench. He didn't even seem to notice that the edge of his shirt was caught on a three-foot-tall bush next to him. Although Nanjundaiah stared at the man, his face was not very clear due to the light from the lamppost behind him. The man looked up a few times, trying to locate some unseen faraway star. Then, when he put his face down on his knee, Nanjundaiah noticed his partly greyed hair. He thought that the man with the glasses must be much younger than himself. As the man sat in this pose, his shadow formed a strange shape. Nanjundaiah walked up and stood beside him. His shadow stood with him; the sound of the footsteps of people who were walking about, whispers. Nanjundaiah simply stood there looking at the man's unseen face.

Nanjundaiah's shadow moved towards the man's shadow. Both the shadows seemed to have known each other for several years, and their lips moved, and their heads nodded slightly. The shadows remained this way for a while, and then they looked at the ground and slowly raised their heads. They looked at each other. Each one could hear the other's struggling breaths. They put their arms on each other's shoulders.

"I wish I could just sleep. But sleep evades me. I've forgotten what that feels like."

"Is that so… Let us think… Can I ask you something?"

"A question? You can ask as much as you want."

"Do you think the answers are so simple and easy?" asked the shadow of the bald-headed face.

"No, would a question give birth to so many little ones if we could get just one correct answer?"

"Is that so? I understood. My problem is that I don't like light," said the shadow of the bald-headed face.

"I got it… Only in the dark do you look at your face in the mirror since it won't be visible. Isn't that right?"

The bald-headed shadow nodded in agreement.

The shadows remained quiet for some time.

"So… same place, tomorrow."

"Ok then… same place, tomorrow."

Once the shadows quieted down, once again, there was a cool breeze from the nearby trees. The usual sound of footsteps in the park could be heard: whispers.

Nanjundaiah walked away with his shadow. From a distance, he turned back and looked. The man hadn't lifted his head from his knee. Nanjundaiah looked up at the sky and realised that it still hadn't rained. He guessed that it might rain that night.

He washed his hands and feet in the bathroom and walked towards his room. His six-year-old grandson Aravind, along with a few other friends, was engrossed in a wrestling match on television.

"I wonder what joy these children get by watching such a terrible thing," said Rekha, picking up the clothes that were strewn around.

"I tell you *ma*, these children would probably feel happier if one of them gets pummelled and falls down dead," said Nanjundaiah solemnly. Rekha instantly looked at him, unable to comprehend the deeper meaning of his words. He looked away, slightly lowering his eyelids, and walked quietly to his room. Lately, he has been plagued with thoughts on how violence is propagated and the way it impacts people. He remained quiet with the unsolvable question as to why love doesn't spread as easily as violence.

Rekha was unsure of the connection between the reference to death that slipped into his words and the way he had recently started talking about the good in death and about the dead. She handed him a big plastic box. He recognised it immediately. He laughed a little and said, "Where did you find it, *ma*... I had given up looking for this."

"Somehow, it was hidden behind the boxes in the kitchen... Isn't it the one that you had been asking for?" she said. "Oh... so then it's still alive?" he said with a smile. On seeing his delight, Rekha felt happy and walked away.

There were many photo negative rolls in the box. They slipped through his fingers and lay strewn around. Later, he picked them up slowly. He picked up one of them and held it against the light. It looked muddled, and he was unable to remember the details. He rolled up all the films and put them into the box. He kept the box on top of the cupboard and let out a small sigh. He leaned against the wall behind the bed and looked outside the window. The occasional thunder did not catch his attention. He saw the lightning a few times.

He heard the scooter stop outside and honk twice. It was a sign that Shivaram was back home. Even as he heard the raindrops falling, Shivaram entered the house, removed his shoes and said, "I was worried that I would get stuck in the rain… luckily I didn't." At the mention of rain, Aravind's friends got up and ran home. "You're still stuck to the TV… Is your *thatha* (grandfather) going to write the test tomorrow?" Shivaram rebuked. Aravind switched off the TV and got up.

"Do you know where the owner of that house lives? Near the cemetery, What else can I do? I went there looking for him. Everything is decided. I've more or less agreed to his conditions. Who wants to live in this terrible house? Not only do we pay the rent, but we also face hundreds of issues. We must move to another house within a week," he said. Rekha had expected this from him, and she replied, "So everything is settled then." He said, "Yes, but when I have just come home in this cold weather, do I also have to ask you for a cup of coffee?" Rekha got up and went to the kitchen.

Only when the rain started pelting against the window did Nanjundaiah realise that it was raining heavily? He closed the window and sat down once again, looking around. The old cot and his suitcase under it, the wooden table, chair, fan, cupboard, the clock on the wall and other things appeared to be dull and trying to say something. He listened to them carefully. The unclear words that he heard sometimes were perhaps theirs, he felt; 'Things, like us who are voiceless, exist only for you, isn't it?' He just sat blankly with his eyes closed for a few seconds. True, they did not have mouths. But it's not false that they had been with him for decades and had shared a bond with him that went beyond words. Truly, they all felt like they had become a part of his body in some ways. Sometimes, when some of them had gone silent, he had felt considerable pain. Now, he was unable to figure out his role in their changing relationship.

The man who put his head down on his knees was present at the park every day. Same stone bench, same posture. Nanjundaiah did not find an opportunity to identify his face from the shadow. But the shadows looked into each other with open eyes, eager to learn about each other's minds, and created their own rhythm. That day, he made up his mind that he must see the man's face; he went to the park two hours earlier than usual. The weight piled on his head by his voiceless, decades-long companions, the load of their words. The man had not yet come to the park. There was nobody else there. Slowly, singles and couples sauntered in. Even then, he did not show up. Nanjundaiah started to feel heavy. His shadow, which was excited and energetic at the beginning, began to slow down and quieten as time passed. Its sight, which spread across the stone bench, began to shrink and became a dot. It reached Nanjundaiah without a word. He was baffled. Then he removed a piece of paper from his pocket and wrote, 'No matter where you are, come tomorrow… you must come. He placed it on the stone bench. When he came the next day, the chit was missing, and the man did not come either. His shadow quietly suffered.

He had effortlessly gathered enough information about the whispered talks between Shivaram and Rekha that had conspired over the past few months. It was about the second child. They didn't seem to have come to a decision on that. 'Time is like clutching onto sand in the palm… they won't realise how quickly it slips away, even without their knowledge. They think that they have everything in their palm, but they will know the reality very late, and nobody can do anything about it,' he felt.

He learnt about the reason behind the new excitement and their movements from Aravind. He said, "*Thatha… thatha…* There is a first-class field near our new house. Didn't you say that you used to play cricket? Please be the umpire for our team. Nobody else is ready, and I've already informed the captain." To which Nanjundaiah replied, "Look, I'm ready anyway… you should not cause trouble by claiming that my decision is wrong, okay?" Aravind said, "Okay, the umpire's decision is final," and ran away shouting. This marks the end of our tenure in this house, thought Nanjundaiah.

Later, as he walked towards the bathroom, Shivaram and Rekha were sitting in the hall discussing the new house. "Only one room has an attached bathroom. If only the other room also had one, both Aravind and *mavayya* could use it," said Rekha. "If we want one more, then the rent is almost twenty-five percent more, you know…" replied Shivaram and lowered his voice as soon as he saw him. Nanjundaiah guessed that they had probably not eaten, engrossed in their talk.

As Nanjundaiah walked back, he heard Shivaram say, "What?... Did you expect me to tell?" Rekha, who noticed that he was within earshot, said, "Quiet, he might listen." He walked up to his room as if he didn't hear a word. Outside, the rain roared louder.

Soon, Rekha came to his room to serve him food, as usual. He had reasons to eat in his room: his desire to avoid the loud noise from the television in the living room and to listen to the passing of time in his quiet room. He just used gestures to convey what he wanted. She said, "We are moving to another house, *Mavayya*…" He raised his head slightly and looked at her. But her mind appeared to be elsewhere. So, their eyes did not meet. Once he finished eating, he washed his plate and kept it back in his room.

When he was still in service, he had only a few friends like Gundappa and Raghunath. He only spoke to them wholeheartedly with trust. That doesn't mean he was always like that. Once, when he asked, "Tell me, how would you measure an hour… Gundu… Raghu…" Gundu replied tersely, "As much as your brain power." But when he insisted on an answer from them, they were clueless. "Nanjundi, you please tell us…" they pleaded. "Look, guys, it is as far as you travel in that time," he said. He pricked a pin and showed them the mark. "The distance from here to each of your homes…" he said. Raghu, who understood this, said, "*Lo*, it's difficult if you fill your head so much… Let us share all that among the three of us, one by three. Get ready and come tomorrow; I will bring the sickle. We will leave the part about taking photos and videos to you, okay?" and laughed. They had continued this topic of conversation over another round of coffee. Nanjundaiah quoted wise persons and reminded them that it is up to each person to get a hold of time and play it according to their wish.

As days passed, he began to lose interest in talking. He began to doubt the compatibility between words and mind. He began to observe that there was no match between them, that the words were mere lies, and he reduced talking. He cultivated that as a habit.

His proficiency in taking photos was appreciated by all. That was his innate skill. During his younger days, it was hidden deep inside him as a mere interest, and then, surprisingly, he grew wings only after he started working and earned some money. The confluence of interest, opportunity, and wherewithal gave way for him to gather information and experiment with photography. He clearly remembered. Like a series of disconnected pictures, the initial days made their mark. It was like a trance, like the gentle union of shadow-light, like bare eyes bereft of everything. He had absolutely no worry about time or money since he had no responsibilities at home. He tried portraits, abstracts, landscapes and so on to figure out what was really close to his heart. His father, who used to repeatedly tell him the importance of time and the kind of personal loss one would face if time was simply wasted, seemed adorable when he finally realised his stupidity and let out a smile from the corner of his lips.

He used to get invites and pressure from several people to take photos. Due to the good quality of the photos, they were periodically published in magazines and newspapers. Friends and others praised his work. When he heard them, his mind would start planning on what to shoot next, forgetting the cost expenses. He was the apple of everyone's eye in his office -- his colleagues, boss and other influential people. Initially, he was eager to fulfil everyone's wishes. A year or two went by with that idealistic view, but then he began to feel overwhelmed. The awards he received once in a while seemed to be only for namesake, and the words of appreciation felt like mere empty talk. Those who posed for the photos did not pay any heed to the expenses involved and thought it was sufficient to just smile and say a few good words about it. It was Raghunath who pointed out that he was being stupid to do this only for appreciation. "I think you are too naive... people who mean nothing asked you to take their photo, and you flew and did it... some others asked you to jump, and you did. Some posed and smiled, and some others laughed behind your back. You are putting your entire salary into someone else's mouth – that's what has happened. Do you realise that?" Nanjundaiah looked foolishly at him. He continued to talk. "Nanjundi, all this will not work out... there should be fair business, but I'm not saying that they must offer you a crown. Now, you have nobody else in your life. How long will you live like this?" he said, looking at the sharp nose on his round face.

Only then did he come down to earth. But gradually, he realised that it wasn't easy for that to become a part of his true nature.

He told Raghunath the same, and later, he laughed and said, "Just because you don't have a craze, you say this… wait until you develop a passion… all the sermon will stop." That is when Gundappa shot his arrow. "Look, you are mad about taking photos, go ahead… take some which give you happiness, along with some others which earn you a few rupees. The loss you incur with one will be compensated by the other. Tell me if I'm wrong," he said, shrugging his shoulders.

"So, what are you trying to say?" he asked, narrowing his small eyes even more.

"Nothing, just contact a few big studios… Follow some public figures like popular people–leaders. Also, if you look for people in the cinema, you will definitely find them other than these two. There's one more golden opportunity…" he paused and shook Nanjundaiah's shoulders to get his attention back from the road where cars and scooters were chasing one another at break-neck speed. Then he said, "Look, the idea is here. Listen… There are many *choultries* (wedding halls) in the city, more or less, and weddings take place throughout the year- they must. Else, what should the marriageable boys and girls do?" Then again, a few seconds later, he said, "You can purchase a video camera also and cover the wedding… get handsomely paid… and you will find plenty of girls to *dove*. If everything looks good, you can get married; you just have to keep your eyes open. There is a way for everything. What do you say, Raghu?" For which Raghu said, "There is no question in what you say… Nanjundi, this is the A, B, and C of business. You will be finished if you forget. Otherwise, you will just have to go from home to office like most others." Nanjundaiah couldn't say much. "Thanks for the suggestions," he said curtly and closed the conversation.

Then, Nanjundaiah didn't talk to anyone in his office for two days. Even Gundappa-Raghunath left him alone. In the midst of all this, Nanjundaiah was trying to find out what he truly felt. Some of the things that he truly believed in grew deeper roots. One – it is shameful to revere someone only for money. Other – there's a big difference between being popular among the masses and popularity. There was no question of him turning away from these two main points. Later, he told the same thing to the two of them in their usual hangout. "No matter what, you are very tough," they said, appreciating him. Before stepping out of the hotel, Gundappa said, "Look, my daughter Radha and son-in-law Ramakrishna are both doctors, as you are aware… They left their government jobs, took a loan and started a nursing home." He gave them an invitation card. Without fail, Nanjundaiah attended the opening ceremony.

Nanjundaiah decided to use photography only as a source of his happiness. He was given the title of being too haughty. He took his own path and won prizes in many competitions. He became quite famous in those circles. He received hundreds of letters of appreciation from people who had the same hobby. There was a file with those letters in the suitcase under his bed. Other than that, he had gained very little in his hobby.

His path in photography was not smooth. Even in clubs and organisations which were known for quality and talent, there were two types of people. One that was capable and another that wasn't. People in both groups constantly fought for recognition and awards. Although it all seemed like fun at the beginning, he began to find it disgusting over time. Their sensitivity did not step outside their creations. Disgusted, Nanjundaiah began to take a greater interest in ordinary matters and ordinary people. He found great satisfaction in that.

It was during one such time that he was introduced to Namratha. One of his photos was published in an exclusive magazine. She was impressed by it and approached him. She researched his attitude even before meeting him. It gave material for their talk. Nanjundaiah felt somewhat special since she had taken him and his photography seriously. He took a keen interest in her.

Namratha, who was overflowing with the excitement of the twenties, was not all that beautiful. But her features were made for the camera. Nanjundaiah was caught up in that mood for several days. She dreamed of becoming a model despite not having any money, influence or contacts. Nanjundaiah encouraged her desires. He even tried to help her to the extent that he could.

It was quite natural for Nanjundaiah to have fallen for Namratha, along with her success and behaviour during the six months he had spent talking in close proximity and contact with her. He felt good since she seemed to be reciprocating his feelings. Hence, the exchange of secrets of their bodies was not unexpected. During those days, he saw Namratha a certain way when he closed his eyes and another way when he opened his eyes. She provided the rainbow's shine to his imagination and dreams.

Right from the beginning, Nanjundaiah was independent at home. He believed that there was complete compatibility with Namratha and nurtured the idea of marrying her; he tried several times to find out what was truly on her mind. But she wasn't clear. He knew that such a relationship had to grow effortlessly and mutually. He felt it was foolish to have such a one-sided wish, and perhaps he hadn't understood her well enough and given up such thoughts.

Gundappa was the first person to sniff it out. Without any hesitation, Nanjundaiah revealed everything. He also asked him to help Namratha reach her goal. Just these words made Gundappa feel very close to Namratha. Within two days, Gundappa burst a bomb. "Your girl's body heat is of high voltage. The joy lingers all day long. I'd never seen such a girl before," he said. As days passed, Gundappa and Namratha began to interact more. Nanjundaiah kept totally away from her. Within three months, as if by some magic, Namratha flew to Mumbai with Gundappa. When Gundappa returned, he just evaded talk about her.

Nanjundaiah and Gundappa never spoke about Namratha. But that day, when her photo was published in the newspaper under the "Missing" section, Nanjundaiah was in no state to speak. He thought that this was probably the result of her relentless pursuit of her goals. "It is not possible to match Namratha's face with anyone else… maybe that's what led to this," said Gundappa, summing it up.

That week, Nanjundaiah received a letter in his office when he was fully engrossed in his work. His eyes filled with surprise and curiosity before opening the envelope. He saw two sentences written by Namratha in the letter – I was unfair to you and me by not understanding you. Please forgive me. The blood rush he felt reading it made him blind, and he couldn't see anything. He recovered in a few seconds and turned over the letter to locate the sender's address, but he couldn't. Then he saw Gundappa standing in front of him. His lips were moving as if he was asking him something. But he couldn't hear a word. Gundappa was intrigued by his unusual behaviour. Nanjundaiah did not reveal his secret even though he asked him several times later. That day, on his way back home, he looked up to find a row of silvery clouds. He saw Namratha's eyes, nose, lips and curls. Overall, the same figure. The same alluring posture. The grace of his favourite maroon saree with black and white circles. Even after reaching home, he was accompanied by the moments of heat and warmth he had spent with her.

The rain had not abated outside. He felt that it was futile to hold the book and put it aside. There was no light in the hall. He guessed that everyone else must have slept. He adjusted his bedsheet. Since he was a little unsettled, he felt that he was far from falling asleep. Somehow, he remembered his daughter Sunitha, who had passed away within one year of marriage and his wife Shyamala. He thought that perhaps his situation would have been different if they were alive. Also, he thought with a deep sigh that if his own financial situation was stronger, he could have made alternate living arrangements for the rest of his days. He now realises that he will never retire again and will give his retirement money to Shivaram to make his own dream of building a house come true. When Raghunath learned about it, he said, "You are doing a stupid thing; that is a worldly statement. On the other hand, you have also gone a step ahead of Yayathi. He only got his youth from his son. But you are trying to perpetuate through your son all the best." His words felt absolutely correct now. He thought of how he had been unaware that everything else seemed to become empty, even as his palms filled up.

He woke up at five-thirty in the morning, and as he was returning from his walk, he found that he had a stiff neck and that it was difficult to turn his head. As usual, he picked up the newspaper from the compound, kept it in the hall, and retired to his room. Earlier, when he had this same issue, he had applied Ayurvedic oil and treated it. He picked up the oil, applied it and rested on the pillow. Soon, he felt better.

As Shivaram-Rekha walked in and out a few times, he felt that their lips looked a bit pursed. Rekha had not even paid much attention towards sending Aravind to school. Aravind kept complaining that something was missing. There was a thick silence for a while after he left. Then Shivaram said, "So, do you say that we should attend to it today itself?" To which Nanjundaiah heard Rekha reply, "*Ree*, you have been so busy with office work and the house that you have been postponing this important thing… if something goes wrong, I'm the one with a problem" Shivaram said, "How can you say that the problem is only yours… it's mine too, not just mine or yours. Both of us have a lot of responsibility, difficult to fulfil it…" Immediately, Rekha replied, "Let's go… no more talk. Let us finish this job today itself. Didn't the doctor tell us to decide without further delay?"

Shortly, as they got ready and were leaving in a hurry, Rekha said, "*Mavayya*, there is *avalakki* for Aravind… please ask him to eat it… I have kept it on top of the table. We will also be back by then." Nanjundaiah observed the clouds gathering in the sky when he went to close the door and thought, 'It must be something important… Let them do what they want. Why should I poke my nose unnecessarily?"

He entered the hall, adjusted his neck and watched the news on TV. Yet, the restlessness that had started earlier did not subside. That is when he realised that he had missed reading the newspaper that day '*Che*! I didn't even think of this. What's wrong with me?' he thought as he looked for his glasses and didn't find them in their usual place. He didn't even find it in the showcase in the hall. He found it on top of the fridge, but when he anxiously tried to pick it up, a small file which was kept beside it fell down. Nanjundaiah wore his glasses and simply glanced at the pages in the file. Immediately, his body felt hot. 'Is this the matter… such foolishness… not a good thing … just don't understand the way this generation thinks… they are tired of only one… don't even want another… they are only smart in reducing their weight…' he thought, and kept it aside helplessly. Then again, he rubbed his neck and looked at the doctor's name and the address of the nursing home. He realised that it was Gundappa's daughter and recollected that he had also attended the inauguration of the nursing home. He got an idea and realised that every second was critical.

First, he called up his office and asked for Gundappa. But the young Raghunath said, "What is it, Nanjundi… you are asking for Gundappa… He is not here. He has gone out on duty. He will be available in the afternoon. You can tell me whatever it is. I'll ask him to call you as soon as he gets back." A slightly disappointed Nanjundaiah said, "I just called for no reason… I'll call back later." Immediately, he called the nursing home. He introduced himself to the receptionist as Doctor Radha's father's friend and said that he needed to speak to her urgently. Within a few seconds, he heard, "Doctor Radha… I know my father talks about you often. How may I help you?" He replied, "My son Shivaram and daughter-in-law Rekha will be coming there. Somehow, you must save it, so please don't take any action until I get there. I cannot explain everything over the phone, please, please…" Radha said, "You are welcome… please come… It will be a pleasure to meet you."

He got ready in two minutes, picked up the umbrella and started. Then he became anxious that Aravind might return home before he got back from the hospital. So, he gave the house key to the neighbour and informed them whatever Rekha had told him.

As he crossed the road outside his house and walked along, he felt a drop fall on his palm, and he looked up. Thick clouds had gathered. By the time he reached the place where he could get autos, it began to drizzle. A young autorickshaw driver refused to take him where he wanted to go. Another driver demanded a double rate, and Nanjundaiah checked his pockets. In that confusion, he had not come prepared for that. "Why am I being stupid…" he thought. He saw the bus approaching, and breathlessly, he made a dash to the bus stop. There were many people there. They thronged the bus as soon as it stopped. He folded up his umbrella, and as he tried to make his way through the crowd, his left chappal came off. He realised it and tried to find it. There was such a jam that he could not even see his own leg. With difficulty, he took out his kerchief and wiped his face. He thought that it was impossible to find the chappal in this chaos; he alighted the bus and felt uncomfortable wearing just one chappal. He removed that, too, right where he stood.

When he got off the stop, he raised his umbrella and walked. He was intrigued at how he kept observing other people's shoes and chappals when he was walking barefoot. Although he could see the nursing home right opposite, he was exhausted by the time he could cross the road in the rain and traffic. He felt as if his work was done just because he had successfully reached the hospital.

He went in, introduced himself and told them that Doctor Radha was expecting him. "Ok, sir, if you can give me your card, I'll give it to the doctor," said the receptionist. A little flustered, Nanjundaiah wrote his name on a piece of paper and gave it. The lady went in and came out and motioned him to go inside.

"Please have a seat… My father has told me a lot about you. I never had the occasion to meet you. Please tell me, what can I do for you?"

"As I said, my son and daughter-in-law may come here…"

"Shivaram and his missus Rekha, right… When I learned that they were your family, I took it up before other cases and took care of them without causing any problems. She said she would take a rest at home; they just left," she said. She picked up the phone and spoke briefly with somebody.

Nanjundaiah looked into Radha's eyes, feeling baffled.

"You said that the abortion must be safe, right? That was also what your son and daughter-in-law wished. I did the same, and it was totally safe; you don't have to worry at all. I truly appreciate you… because these days, it is common for couples to opt to have a single child. But it is rare that you, too, have supported it…"

"What I mean to say... you should have until I came..." said Nanjundaiah in a mellowed tone as he went pale.

"You see, in the hurry... I forgot to tell them that you were coming here anyway, and everything is fine now."

"Okay... what's left for me to say anymore... thanks," he said, realising the futility of expressing his wish and got up, avoiding Doctor Radha's face. She was alarmed when she saw his facial muscles twitch and asked him, "Anything wrong?"

"No... nothing..." he said and walked away. He stood at the doors of the nursing home, trying to digest the fact that there was no hope of saving the baby; it was too late to request the doctor not to abort the baby. It was raining heavily. Since he didn't feel like standing there, he stepped out without realising that he had to open the umbrella and got completely soaked in the rain. In a state of confusion, he looked up, and a drop of rainwater fell into his right eye, and everything began to appear watery. After reaching home, he had no chance of bringing it up, as Shivaram-Rekha were immersed in conversation regarding the move as if nothing untoward had happened.

The next day, the preparation to move to the new house began. Since they had lived in the same house for six years, it took them longer to throw the unwanted items away than packing the required items. Nanjundaiah began organising his personal belongings. When he shook the suitcase to empty it, all the contents fell out. A few cockroaches, too, fell out and ran helter-skelter. There were decades-old letters about awards and felicitations. They had turned brown now. With narrowed eyes, he read a few letters. True, it brought back memories. When he tried to recall, he saw himself as one of the audience. He also skimmed through other letters. They belonged to people totally unknown to him. He didn't feel a thing. He just threw them into a corner.

He sat for a while, gazing absentmindedly at the edge of the faded wall. Then he shook his head slowly and got up as if he was very weak. He took each of the negative rolls out of the plastic boxes, held them up against the light and checked. Some rolled away. Only a few countable ones were worthy of grabbing earnest attention. He kept those on the table. He put the remaining in the box. He got up, took a deep breath, and stretched himself on the bed.

He couldn't sit still. He kept looking at the corner, the box and the table. He got up again and put those that were lying in the corner into the box. He put on a shirt over the same *panche* (dhothi) that he was wearing, picked up the box and walked across the room. From there, he turned back and looked at the table again. He hesitated, went back in and stuffed the remaining ones into the box. He went out to the dimly lit street and threw them all into the trash at the corner, gulped and stood there for a few seconds. At that time, he was unaware of all the surrounding noise and looks. As he started walking back, he suddenly thought of Namratha.

As time passed by, he lost track of whether it was evening or night. Nobody seemed to be home. He got up to close the front door. As he walked up, a hand stopped him. It was accompanied by the jingling of bangles and the sound of footsteps inside the house. Nanjundaiah stepped back and looked. His eyes scrunched up.

He recognised the person who was covered up to the neck in a shawl. It was Namratha.

"May I come in...?"

They simply smiled. Hesitantly, their eyes met. They didn't know what to say as they stood there. He then stared at her. He was sure that this was the same Namratha. Once he caught his breath, he walked towards the room. Namratha followed him.

Nanjundaiah sat leaning against the wall, and Namratha sat in the chair opposite him as they began to talk. They must have understood each other.

He heard Aravind's voice coming from outside the house. Nanjundaiah got up to open the door. Namratha was right behind him. Before she stepped out of the door, Nanjundaiah asked, "When will you come next?" She replied, "I'm always ready." Nanjundaiah then noticed the part of the saree below the shawl. Instantly, he remembered. That was the same saree that he had seen the other day. After two years since she had gone missing, her family received her dead body. A reluctant Nanjundaiah had gone there along with Gundappa, who insisted. In the short time that he stood there, quietly breathing, the white saree with the black border on her body caught his eye.

Aravind ran inside. "Make way *thatha* (grandpa)... want to watch cartoon," he said, switching on the television. Shivaram and Rekha followed him.

They were all set to move to the new house. That day, Shivaram and Rekha were bustling about. Aravind's face was full of happiness. But the tempo truck did not come on time. Finally, dark clouds collected in the sky. This resulted in anxiety. Shivaram had reached a point where he was ready to pounce at anyone who tried to talk to him. He rebuked Aravind a few times, too. Nanjundaiah felt, 'The state of mind is more important than the house', and just sat quietly watching the hours go by.

Once the tempo arrived in the afternoon, everything happened quickly. Somehow, Aravind seemed to be dull. Nanjundaiah called him and asked, "Why the sad face?" To which he replied, "I just couldn't find my box of marbles." As soon as Nanjundaiah replied, "Oh, that… somehow it got mixed up with my things. I'll give it to you later x." He was delighted.

It began within half an hour of getting all the things. A roaring rain that could set all the things adrift began to pour. The road and the footpaths were drowned in the rainwater.

Only the following morning did Nanjundaiah see the man living next door. He appeared to be around his own age. He was puzzled that his eyes, nose, mouth and overall figure looked somewhat familiar and unfamiliar. Their eyes met three times. The strands of hesitation dissolved. Nanjundaiah slowly approached him and said, "Hello…" and caught his attention. "You remind me of a friend…" he began, then they exchanged their names, city, school and other information. Immediately, Nanjundaiah said, "Hey, you are our Raju, right?" Even before he completed the sentence, the man said, "How are you, Nanjundi…" immediately addressing each other in singular terms. They calmed down after the initial excitement of the chance meeting and went to Rajappa's house for a heart-to-heart talk. First, they talked about their personal experiences since they parted after high school.

"Even after ten years of marriage, somehow, we both just did not get along. Now I'm on my own. She is on her own… For some reason, we did not have any children. In a way that was right," Rajappa talked about his wife. Nanjundaiah nodded his head as if in agreement. Rajappa just sat there silently for a few seconds and then said, "But look, Nanjundi, living alone like this feels as if a *nagaari* (type of drum) is beating close to the ear, always. There is no escape from this. It is like being punished with a triple life term." He then scratched his forehead with his finger ring. Then, they sat quietly for a while. Later, when they continued their conversation, they were surprised that they shared their worldly dealings from the remaining half century within a mere half an hour. They laughed, looking at each other, then leaned back, stared and again laughed. They sat in silence for a while.

Then Rajappa said, "What is this… everything is empty… its all over right, Nanjundi?" And Nanjundaiah replied, "That's just how it is… it's impossible for anything else to happen."

As they reminisced about their childhood days, they once again began to relive each and every incident and its details. They lost track of time. As they kept looking, they realised that other than the simple happiness and pains of their childhood, everything else was a waste and meaningless. They sat talking only about that. Only when Aravind came up and said, "*Amma* is calling you for lunch, *thatha*", did Nanjundaiah laugh and say, "I found you. Now I'm not worried anymore, Raju." And he walked away.

From the very next day, Nanjundaiah and Rajappa's routines changed. Even though he had a family, Rajappa was now alone, and Nanjundaiah was facing an adverse situation in the family; they both completely stopped thinking about it.

He craved to pull the good old days even closer. "Come Nanjundi," said Rajappa, who took him to the cycle shop. They rented two cycles and pedalled, racing each other, just like in the olden days. When one got tired, the other would tease, and the other way round, they would become elated. Both of them took days to recover from the body pain due to this. But their joy was not reduced.

Then, they got ready once again. "Nanjundi, we must play marbles… I must see if you still have the same magic in your fingers. I went around this place once. I didn't get any marbles," he said. "I'll be right back," Nanjundaiah said and went into his house. As he picked up and held the faded box of marbles against his chest, he heard laughter. Not knowing the source of the voice, he looked around and thought, "Did Aravind come… if so, we can include him in the game." He didn't see Aravind as he looked about. He joined Rajappa hurriedly. Rajappa shook the box of marbles and felt goosebumps. He looked around and said, "It's very constricting here, Nanjundi… come, let's go to the high school playground." Rajappa also looked up and observed that the light had dimmed just before they left for the playground. "Very dense clouds have gathered, Nanjundi… let's play tomorrow," he said; Nanjundaiah gave a deaf ear to it.

After they reached the school grounds, and before starting the game, Rajappa asked, "What do your knees say, Nanjundi? Are the batteries charged enough to play for half an hour?" Nanjundaiah laughed in reply and did two sit-ups, looking at him.

Like before, they began to prepare everything. First, they made a round hole, checked its perimeter and shape, and nodded. They fixed the other distances by the feet. Then they opened the box and picked out the marbles. When they spread them out, the marbles turned into small children. They could see the spring of excitement, shining light from their eyes, and bounty of eagerness in them. Nanjundaiah-Rajappa stroked their heads, patted their backs and let them out to play. Is there a limit for children's play?... One joining the other, one chasing another, scrunching the face if hurt and jumping with joy in case of a win. Even Nanjundaiah-Rajappa became one in all their movements and other activities. Sometimes, they pulled them closer and wiped their sweaty necks-foreheads. When they did that, the odour of the sweat hit Nanjundaiah-Rajappa, and their noses quivered. All this made them shout, scream and howl.

Later, they were lost in the game, losing track of time. Sometimes, their shouts and exclamations attracted other people's attention. It began with one or two people, and gradually, they were surrounded. As their game became more and more colourful, the people standing around them were not only surprised but also found it entertaining.

As the raindrops fell, their game became more intense. When Nanjundaiah's fingers flexed and hit the marble, which was not just one but even two meters away, Rajappa jumped with joy. "What a shot... what a shot..." he said, clapping and rejoicing. Some of the people also shouted, "*Shabash*", "*Wah re wah*", and "Good shot", and Nanjundaiah stood up and looked around. Youngsters, elders, children – they were all there. In the evening light, the drizzle formed a backdrop, with water flowing down several faces, postures, and twilight – all this, along with the surrounding view, looked like Still Photographs. A smile appeared on his lips. His mind dangled and dipped in several places and came up shining. For a few seconds, he was lost, and only when Rajappa patted his back did he get back into the game.

As soon as the rain picked up, all the people standing around left. But their game did not stop.

Nonstop, it continued... play... rain... rain... play...

Rathasapthami

An hour's walk just before sunrise keeps the body somewhat fit. As Prabhakar stepped out to enjoy the feel of the smooth breeze on his skin, it fleetingly caressed his eyelids and knocked to check if all was well. He bumped into his friends. The walking pace with them changed with the pace of their talk in various directions. The last night's news, today's hell in politics, and reaching a resolution that Bangalore is no different from any city in Bihar. He would hang all these on the branches of the trees on his way back home. He would normally take about an hour and a half to get ready to go to the press. He had to read the newspaper, take a bath, and eat his breakfast within that time. Somehow, this hurry has become the normal routine these days. But what else could it be? Bangalore is such a swing of likes and dislikes.

As he was perusing the newspaper, "*Ree*, you've got a call," said his wife, Malini. He gestured, asking who it was. She covered the mouth of the receiver and said, "Shivaraman," for which he waved his hand. She said, "He has stepped out for a walk… I'll inform him when he returns, ok?" Then she put the phone down and walked away to pack her son Vishesh's lunch box; he was studying in the second standard. Prabhakar often did this since he was unable to complete the work given to him by Shivaraman and other such people despite his best efforts. But when talking to people who owed him money, who owed him some balance amount, the government employees who would say, 'Please give us first,' without passing the bill, and lately, even with the private company employees, he would speak in colourful tone.

His father, Shankaraiah, who was almost due for retirement, had taken some days off to organize all the documents and letters required for his retirement. Simultaneously, he was also planning to set up a consultancy on quality control in production to avoid the burden of spending time.

He said, "We must pay the last instalment of the LIC policy this time. Since you are headed that way, pay it," and gave him all the details of the policy. Later, he said, "So, why haven't you taken insurance yet? By the way, I've been telling you to insure your press, scooter, the TV at home and everything. What have you done about it?"

"I've got it done for the scooter… otherwise the police won't spare me. The rest will have to wait."

Prabhakar's printing press was located in the Jayanagar area, on a crossroad adjacent to a main road. Shankaraiah had taken a loan from the bank to procure all the required machinery for offset printing and set it up for him. At that time, Prabhakar had been excited to start a job that he had craved for. But he was a bit disturbed by asking his father for financial support to do it. He often wished that he had started it with his own earnings. He comforted himself with the realization that wishes and earnings are not easily fulfilled. So, he also approached some of his friends for help in raising the seed money. But since they were also financially poor like him, invariably, he had accepted his father's help as he had no other alternative.

Especially on the day he got the machinery for the press, it was like a feast for his eyes. It felt as if the day would never end, *Arre*! And the day ended already. That was the day he realized the true brightness of light. Suddenly, a smile was playing on his lips, and he looked up at the sun. The light rushed into his eyes, forcing him to shut them. The rays that fell on his closed eyelids burst into an array of blue, green, yellow and white colours inside his eyes; the fleeting sight of the spectrum of colours kept the smile on his lips. Then he unpacked each item, cleaned and arranged it neatly. Suddenly, a memory flashed before his eyes: a time when his mother Lalithamma used to draw elaborate rangoli on the day of the Rathasapthami festival; as a young boy, he used to stand and watch keenly as she used the rangoli powder and colourful chalk pieces to draw the Sun's chariot, with a flag, and ropes to rein the horses and so on. Just like the horses of the Sun's chariot galloped forward, he believed that all these machines would help him succeed in the path of progress. With this belief, he later set up desktop publishing to cater to Kannada, English and other languages.

Shankaraiah decided to spend half a day in quality control consultancy work after retirement. The other half of the day, he thought of spending some quiet time at home. That way, he wished to make the most out of everything. "Do it, sir; you'll save a lot of energy," he would tell people who are close to him. He hated any kind of meandering talk, lectures, and especially meaningless and aimless shower of words of the politicians. Sometimes, people would approach him and ask him to give a talk on the Quality of Industrial Production. He always refused. Once, someone close to him took the liberty and asked him to give a talk on the "Standards of Politics", and it really irritated him.

Prabhakar was very excited in the initial days of starting the press. He employed four boys and a few others on a part-time basis to work on the DTP. He, too, learnt to work on the DTP along with them. But he often faced trouble from them, and the work suffered. To meet the expenses of running the press, he had to rely only on the job work. The occasional small bookwork orders from the private sector brought him more joy than the clients. He had learnt to design his orders based on their objective and content. He was well-known for that. But he was eager to take on larger orders from the government departments. If the private sector had one type, then there were a hundred types. He realized that in the circle of their tenders, orders, bills and cheques, it was difficult to progress. There was no place for sensitivity there; he became aware that even after trying to grasp their conventional ways, there were many unexpected obstacles, and the overall progress was minimal. But he had decided that he would only pursue Printing, the only career that he knew. He was very fond of Venku, who would work quickly and efficiently on the DTP jobs in the press. He would also deliver them after work.

That day, Prabhakar went to get a bill passed in one of the government departments. He was pacing up and down the corridor, with no natural light outside the room, lit only by the dim electric bulbs. He was chiding himself that he wouldn't even be acknowledged for coming empty-handed. Just then, a person who stepped out of the room and passed by Prabhakar stepped back and stared at him. Perhaps they both recognized each other's faces and features.

"You… you are Prabhakar, right?" he looked at and asked the round-faced, thick-haired, burnt reddish skin tone, average build with a height of five and three Prabhakar.

"Yes… are you Naganna?"

Both their eyes shone, and exchanged camaraderie. The happiness spread into a smile. For a moment, the surrounding people disappeared, and they felt exhilarated.

Soon, they were sitting and sipping coffee together in a hotel. Naganna keenly listened to Prabhakar as he narrated his story.

"Consider your job done."

"What do you mean?"

"I am with Minister Jawarappa now," said Naganna.

"With him?!"

Naganna told him briefly about himself. Then, "Our *sahib* entrusts all the work of his near and dear ones, along with this and that to me. I assign it to such officers on his behalf. I meet them if it is very important." He placed his empty coffee cup on the table.

Prabhakar wondered about the unexpected encounter with the strange professional world and whether the person sitting across the three-foot table was the same Naganna that he had known earlier. He had the same square burnt red face, small forehead, and slightly flat nose, only fuller cheeks than before. But maybe a few cultivated changes in behaviour, he thought. Naganna noticed Prabhakar struggling to string his words and said, "What, man, you seem to be low. Take some good medicine to regain your strength. If you don't know, let me know. I'll arrange it for you." This extreme display of affection instantly created soft music in Prabhakar's heart and made him smile.

"All the excitement becomes decrepit just by passing each day and acquiring the ordinary luxuries of life. There's no question of anything else."

Prabhakar and Naganna were classmates at Chitradurga College. Prabhakar's house was close to *Rangayyana bagilu,* and Naganna lived near *Ekanatheshwari* temple. The surprisingly close friendship between the slightly shy Prabhakar and a bit too bold Naganna was quite special. Once Prabhakar had read T. R. Subba Rao's (popularly known as TaRaSu) novel, '*Hamsa Geethe*', and was completely in awe of it. Is it even possible to understand the depth of Hulluru Srinivasa Jois's mind who narrated the story of Bhairavi Venkata Subbaiah, who cut his tongue out to avoid singing in front of the Nawab, to TaRaSu and urged him to write this novel? As he narrated this incident at midnight, on a bench in *Rangayyana bagilu*, Naganna's wonderstruck face looked like a half-drawn portrait. "Even if he was offered half the kingdom, Venkatasubbaiah refused to sing, right Naganna… there's a price for wealth… but is it possible to set a price for loyalty?" he had said.

As always, Naganna won the elections as the president of the college student association, which is a symbol of his organizing capacity. People were impressed by Naganna's speeches. But the pamphlets, posters, banners, slogans and so on were all designed by Prabhakar.

"*Guru*, write down the details of the work for which you have come now," said Naganna as the cell phone in his pocket started to ring. As he spoke in a tame manner, Prabhakar wrote the details on a piece of paper.

"But Naganna, earlier you were supporting Narasimha Murthy and his party… but now…" said Prabhakar, probing.

"Yes. It's true. I supported him for a few years, but what should I do? I had to do this since there was no other way. Other than him, everything else is crooked. When it comes to the party, is it possible to say one is better than the other? In short, I can say that *kanchanam karya siddhi* (money makes work possible). Do you say all this is wrong? Tell me, what has been your experience so far?"

"But how are you doing now?"

"Truth be told, I was suffering for one reason earlier, and now I am suffering for a different reason." When the phone rang again, "It is election time…" said Naganna and got up.

As Naganna told-Prabhakar went to Jawarappa's house to meet him. There was a long line of cars and other vehicles filled with desires. The people there, who were standing inside the compound and standing or sitting here and there, had anxious longing flowing in their blood. Jawarappa saw Prabhakar for just a moment and said, "Naganna has given me all the information. You, please help him a bit. I'd like to try you out and decide.

Naganna will tell you everything else. You can meet me anytime you want."

Prabhakar did not take too long to gather Naganna's requirements. The eighteen years of gap between the two comrades suddenly disappeared. There was more or less the same intensity and involvement as before. The reason behind all the stress was the upcoming elections.

Jawarappa had also given Prabhakar some work in his office. People's movement, the bustle of the party workers, the behaviour of leaders at different levels, and the various dialects in the Kannada language were all new to him. Somehow, they all seemed to be on a hot pan. Prabhakar had brought about a radical change in the font size, style, face and colour in the new pamphlets and posters, and not only did Naganna jump with joy, but Jawarappa himself had summoned Prabhakar and said, "You have a good future," with a twinkle in his eyes. He was excited by this and met him again after two days. "Please take a look at these new kinds of slogans, as you had asked," he said and showed half a dozen slogans that he had penned. He read each of them twice and finally marked one of them and said, "I liked this very much. I will send it to high command," and patted his shoulders.

Jawarappa was in a quandary. If he did not step in a unified manner, he would fall into a pit. During some rare solitary moments, he revisited his journey and said to himself, "This is the face that our people have given me. It is their mirror, and they can look at it. I don't have the freedom to feel disgusted about it."

Naganna had arranged some work for Prabhakar that fetched him more profit than he could possibly imagine. Out of those, some took the straight road, and some crooked. Prabhakar knew that Naganna had some other leverage in return. Even as he was figuring out the requirements of each of them, he was bombarded with more work. He felt like there were suddenly windows here, there, everywhere, and doors opened up through which bright sunlight streamed in and spread the light everywhere, and the winds of work pressure swept right behind it. The immediate impact of all this was a disturbance in his daily routine. He had committed to each and every opportunity that came his way, irrespective of the timelines. There was no scheduled time to go home. Often, Lalithamma would say, "What kind of work is this, where you don't have timely food and lose your peace of mind due to lack of sleep?" To which Prabhakar would reply, "First, hard work; peace comes later." He felt like he was transgressing all the boundaries of his imagination and floating in the breeze along the jubilant roads. Lately, however, he has been drowned in displeasure – the support from his family, including his father, mother, and wife, did not match his expectations. Now, Shankaraiah had to take on the responsibility of dropping Vishesh to school. Just like in a few earlier instances, Prabhakar hadn't reached home in time to take Vishesh to the exhibition as he had promised earlier. He created such a ruckus that they were all worried. Malini was exhausted after pacifying him and refused to talk to Prabhakar the next day. But Prabhakar did not take this incident very seriously.

That day, an executive of a company who appreciated Prabhakar's work gifted him with a somewhat beautiful doll. Prabhakar thought that Vishesh might really like the doll. Since it was already midnight by the time he reached home, he decided to give it to him the next morning. Malini was already asleep after dinner. Somehow, he was drawn to her sleeping posture. He was slowly overcome with emotion, as he felt like he was looking at her beauty for the first time, and wondered if this was truly his wife, Malini. He felt that if he tried anything at this time, she would get enraged, and he quietly lay down beside her. Within a few seconds, he heard a voice, "What is this? Why did you become quiet?" Prabhakar sat up and looked in the direction of the voice. He could only see the doll that he had kept on the table in the corner of the room. Malini, too, woke up feeling a bit flustered. Even as she asked, "Who is it, *ree*?" they heard the same words again. Then they realized. It was the doll talking. They looked at each other. As they walked towards it, they felt a mix of emotions, mostly a strange kind of happiness. They waited a few seconds, hoping it would say something more.

"I felt like it said something?!"

"Didn't it sound like a child's voice?"

"No, I don't think so. It sounded like an adult," said Prabhakar. But the doll had changed their present state of mind.

The next day, the talking doll became the favourite of the entire family. The main event was its naming ceremony. Finally, they named it "Puttu" as per Vishesh's wishes. The doll would laugh and walk when they called out its name, creating waves of happiness in them. Prabhakar left in a hurry due to work pressure. Vishesh was delighted to have a companion to talk to. He spent all the time with it as soon as he returned home from school. He was enthralled by its words. For Shankaraiah and Lalithamma, who watched the days roll by uneventfully from sunrise to sunset, this brought about a change. The laughing and dancing doll that initially made everyone feel good began to express its wants in an irritating way within a few days. Instead of playing with whatever was given to it that day, it created a ruckus demanding a horse. After waiting a while, Shankaraiah called Prabhakar at his press and informed him about it. On his way back from work, he picked up a wooden toy horse from the fourth block. Jayanagar tied it to his scooter and brought it home. On seeing this, Puttu became extremely active. It climbed on it and happily rocked it back and forth. Then it jumped out and lovingly kissed all over Prabhakar's face. Although this brought things back to normalcy for the others, Vishesh was just not amused. He was fuming all day. Later, Puttu spent most of the day riding the horse. Some mornings, it would watch the rangoli that Lalithamma made just outside the main door. It would not be very demanding then. Lalithamma would smile at it. She would call Vishesh and say, "Come and see what Puttu is doing." After a few days, it somehow found the rangoli box of colourful chalk pieces. It drew reins on the wooden horse with it. Since then, it began to ride the horse with extreme enthusiasm and displayed a lot of attitude.

Initially, when it would only walk around at home, it had torn the pages off Shankaraiah's book on "Quality Control in Industrial Production" and rendered them useless, spoiling all his tools right before his eyes. For a few seconds, Shankaraiah just couldn't believe his eyes. But slowly, he reconciled with the fact. He didn't talk to anyone for the next three days. But another day, Puttu started ringing the bell that Shankaraiah used when he lit the incense during prayer and did *mangalarathi* (prayed with a lit-up wick) to the photo of a prominent leader in Jawarappa's party, which was hung in the hall. Vishesh jumped, clapped, and laughed with excitement at seeing this. Shankaraiah heard the bell ring and came to check. He was shocked at the sight and stood rooted to the spot. But Malini couldn't control herself. When she tried to snatch the bell from Puttu, it just gave her a menacing stare, and she continued with the job. She dragged and pushed it into the room and locked the door. They all looked at each other and moved away. Yet, the sound of the ringing bells could be heard from the room. Later, everyone at home, except for Prabhakar, who also heard about the incident, spent the entire day as if the house was mourning.

Puttu, who used to talk like a young boy in the beginning, soon began to speak like an adult. Now, the people at home were surprised to see how Puttu's eyes, eyebrows and lips synchronized perfectly with the ups and downs of its words. Sometimes, its eyes appeared black, and sometimes they appeared blue. At first, they were all happy to observe these changes, but soon, it began to poke its nose in every aspect. Not only did their family seem to somehow be aware of all the other happenings, but they also all tried to keep away from it. But Prabhakar never talked about putting it away. It encouraged him further to race forward in the path that he had chosen. He had clearly identified his place and his loyalties, which he wanted to safeguard.

Prabhakar had to ensure that he made arrangements to deliver the completed work order, or he had to throw a party for some people who were directly responsible for getting a corporate order, or he had to meet Naganna or visit Jawarappa or his office and so on – due to such work commitments, he usually returned home only after midnight. Although they were used to it, Malini suffered the most due to this. Lately, she was also fed up, so she laid dinner on the table, helped Vishesh with his homework, and completed other chores in the house. But she still had the job of opening the door for Prabhakar late at night. These days, she had found a solution to that, too. She locked the front door. When he came home, they had made an arrangement so that he unlocked the door and entered the house.

Puttu, who used to sleep anywhere earlier, began to insist on sleeping only in their bedroom. Just to keep it quiet, she would allow it to sleep on her bed until Prabhakar came home. Later, Prabhakar would sweet talk to Puttu and convince him to move to the top of the table. Malini was very annoyed by this. She complained that he talked more to Puttu than she did. But these days, it had started a different tune. Puttu did not listen to Prabhakar when he asked it to sleep separately. It insisted on sleeping with them. That day, all their efforts to convince Puttu were wasted. Malini, who finally allowed it to sleep on her bed, sat at the bed's edge all night. Prabhakar, who was exhausted, fell asleep. At daybreak, everything went back to normal. But this incident did not stop there, and they had to listen to Puttu every day. Sometimes, when Malini was half asleep, she couldn't figure out whether the body pressing against her was Prabhakar or Puttu, but with disgust, she would get up from the bed and sleep on the floor. Somehow, she felt afraid when Puttu grinned and stared at her sometimes. She thought hard and asked Prabhakar to give her a divorce and live with Puttu, or she herself would go ahead and file for divorce. As days passed, it started acting up more.

Prabhakar's throat felt parched whenever he heard about the incidents related to elections in other cities. He knew many people in and out of the party office. Many times, Jawarappa used to say,

"Consult Prabhakar… do as he says". People could not accept this, and it gave way to a spark of jealousy. Even Naganna was not exempt from this. At such times, he would look at Prabhakar from head to toe judgingly.

That night, Prabhakar, Venku, and others had a lot of work to do. They packed idlis from a nearby hotel and ate, and it was three in the night when they finally finished work, rubbing their eyes. Tying the bundles, Venku said, "I want a day off tomorrow, sir." Lately, Prabhakar had not consented twice when he asked. When he saw his pale face even while asking, he said, "Okay… I will deliver it myself. You can go just for one day."

The sun was already up when Prabhakar, who hadn't slept well for a week, woke up. Puttu, who had created a ruckus at night, continued as soon as it saw him. It had just one demand for the past two days. It wanted him to take it to Jawarappa's house. "Why… isn't the present situation enough?" said Malini with a grumpy face. Yet, unable to refuse, Prabhakar agreed. Shankaraiah raised his eyebrows. Vishesh, unable to fathom the entire situation, walked up and down, looking at everyone's faces.

As Prabhakar got ready in a hurry, Puttu sat on the pillion seat of the scooter. He picked up the printed bundles from the press. As he drove, the heat of the hot sun bounced off the road and hit his eyes. As he went further, he stopped for the red light at South End Circle. He saw a large hoarding of Jawarappa on the roadside. But the font of the words did not match. He parked the scooter there and went up to the hoarding to take a closer look. Puttu followed him. The hoarding had a photo of Jawarappa giving a speech, and the field in front of him was full of people:

men, women and children. As he stood there, a wave of applause from these people reached Prabhakar. He, too, began to clap, and Puttu joined him. The light turned green at the circle, and many vehicles behind him began honking. Prabhakar hurried back to his scooter, started it and moved forward. He turned back and looked suspiciously. Somehow, Puttu seemed to be in his place. As he was speeding down J C Road, he saw many people spread out across the road. Just like in other places, the road was lined with buntings, posters, and banners for Jawarappa and other candidates. As he drove further, he heard some screaming and shouting in hoarse voices. As he approached the screams, he saw a few people tearing down Jawarappa's posters. By then, he had already come close to them. Yes! Hadn't he seen some of them in the party office? He wondered why they were doing this as he stopped his scooter and tried to put on the stand. Perhaps something from below must have hit it. The scooter fell; Puttu also fell along with the loosely tied bundles. Jawarappa's election campaign pamphlets from the bundles scattered everywhere. A few people standing there noticed this. One of them picked it up in a hurry and said, "Hey, look at Jawarappa's *chela* (servant)…" Another one shouted, "Even after all this, he is going to hold the bucket for the *thayiganda*." People crowded around him. Prabhakar found their behaviour very strange. Weren't they all Jawarappa's followers just yesterday? He wondered as someone poked him in the ribs. He turned to see a few wide, angry eyes and crazy laughter. In all this pandemonium, his eyes searched for Puttu. But he couldn't see it. Immediately, it was followed by a *thaiya thakka thaiya* sound. "That Jawarappa sold himself out, changed the party and has absconded… Here, you've come to scratch his ass, *xloudeki loudike*." Another man picked up the pamphlets and tried to thrust them into Prabhakar's mouth. When Prabhakar tried to lift up his head, the sunlight blinded him. He found it difficult to stand. In this chaos, people stamped on Puttu and its hands, legs and faces were shattered and scattered all around. One of them who collected these pieces felt something move, and he tried to piece them back together. All the pieces fell into place in a natural way. The face began to shine a bit, and the lips curved into a smile. Later, it began to talk.

A Visit To The River

*A*lthough we've been sitting here in anticipation for the last three days, doesn't it feel as if we've been here for many years? Look at how quickly we blend into any place. We have now become very familiar to those who looked at us with great curiosity and doubt just a few days back.

Now, I am terribly distressed over Sridhara. I hadn't expected the state of affairs to become so dangerous. This situation was totally unexpected, especially for you.

They call it a *kallahole* (sinkhole). It is difficult to determine the spots where the sand has sunk in, which created deep pits. A vast difference can be observed within a distance of just two feet. This river is special in a way; it turns and flows from the west to the south. The stone *mantapa* (an ornamental structure) in the middle was submerged in the water when I came with Sridhara. Now, there is just enough water to create a small pond next to it; it has become a source of fish for fishermen to catch. I find it surprising to find them sitting there for hours together, waiting to catch the fish – how about you?

With things being so, it is a little difficult not to get carried away by the effect of the setting sun. I've become hardened by sitting here, exposed to the winds for the past three days. Perhaps, if

I hadn't taken such an important decision in my life, such a circumstance would never have occurred. But could I do so? Tell me.

Look behind. There's an old, dilapidated house where the plastering has fallen off the walls. Further back, on the top, lies the temple *kalasha* (ornamental metal cover). Only when you see it can you infer that a temple that was so majestic during Jakanachari's time is now in such bad condition. Am I right? The staircase that we took to come here and sit down was very narrow back then. It has been widened now. See the road bridge in front of us and the rail bridge beyond that. Between them, on the other bank of the river, is the waterworks. What is seen beyond the sand dunes is a factory. They have their own boat club. I saw and explored all that when I came with Sridhara. He was extremely happy. But, as usual, he spoke only a few words now and then. He gave just one answer if I asked him ten questions. You know, Suddenly, he gets moody.

Here we are, counting minutes, anxious. Those people walking down the road bridge are not weighed down by time. The strange thing is we are waiting for the unexpected. Isn't it? Yesterday, when we saw a shirt washed ashore among the reeds and I let out a muffled scream, you must have been extremely worried. Do you agree?

When Sridhara came with his cricket team to play a league match, I accompanied him. As we were newlyweds, the team members left Sridhara and me to ourselves. That was the first time we both saw the river. Sridhara's craze for the river was surprising. You should have seen him standing in it for hours together, although he didn't know how to swim. He asked me to bathe in it. I declined. But he insisted until I relented.

"Bhageerathi should come here every day, Sir, to witness the roaring river. As far as I remember, there was just two feet of water when the bridge and the arch had to be closed. During such days, it is such a thrill to see the water rise in the morning and evening, Sir," said the manager of the guest house.

Sridhara was listening wide-eyed. I was amazed. "How would a man who is so excited about a river react when he sees the sea?" I asked him. "That's not the point. Look, there are boulders on this bank and sand on the other side; here's a temple, and there is filth; the parallel road bridge and rail bridge, and along with this mix-up, the sweetness of the river water. The sea doesn't give this kind of unique experience," replied Sridhara. I had tried to find the strand of his character behind such keen observation. I had looked at his lean face with sharp eyes. His words of excitement had the glow of gentle sunrays - a peaceful, comforting experience.

It is fun to imagine the grim look on a person's face when he waits for the ball while playing a cricket match, especially one who speaks in this manner. I don't understand why I get so anxious when Sridhara begins to bat. Perhaps I have become more serious than him. It looks very curious, doesn't it? His forward stretch, square drive, off-drive, on-drive poses remain like movie stills in my mind. He batted well in the match that was played in this place. At such times, it is very nice to see his shining eyes on his dull face. It gives me a kind of satisfaction: a sense of pride in winning. I think I looked at him just to see if a smile escaped from his face despite his tiredness in making the run. I felt as if his personality expanded all of a sudden, and I was caught in its attraction - do you feel that this is a bit too much? Maybe, But I'm confiding in you without hiding anything.

I'm sorry, the sequence of events that I'm narrating to you now may be a bit jumbled due to the pressure of the current situation. I'm just telling you as the memories come to mind. Is that okay?

What? Oh, Are you asking me about that one? Watermelon and muskmelon are grown in those squares. When the green watermelon is cut open, it has a blood-red colour inside. Even though it is cool and tasty to eat, it produces a lot of heat in the body.

The next day's incident is unforgettable. As Sridhara and I were bathing at that spot, a couple with a baby and two middle-aged men came there. They must have been picnickers. They sat down, talking for about ten minutes. Later, the men entered the water. The woman sat on the bank with the playful baby. It appeared as though none of them were as crazy about the river as Sridhara. The men finished bathing and came up onto the bank, except for the woman's husband. She kept the snacks ready and called out to her husband. She called out twice thrice. Sridhara had become one with the river and didn't notice any of this. The man kept saying, just a minute, just a minute while flailing his arms and legs as if he were swimming. Then, probably, something flashed in his mind. He moved ten to fifteen steps ahead. In a second, he disappeared. Everyone was shocked. The woman screamed.

The men who had accompanied them ran towards the spot. A localite warned them not to go there. It seemed as if the sand at that spot had sunk in. As he rushed there, Sridhara and I ran back to the bank. This almost cinematic incident sent a small shiver deep inside me. "Why are you looking at me like that? Did you get alarmed, too?"

There were not any good swimmers there who could be of help. Everyone was left shivering in the chaos. The localite dived into the place where the man had disappeared and surfaced. He dived over and again and came up. He got tired of holding his breath, shook his hands, and returned to the banks. Everything was finished in just a minute or two. By then, somebody had brought a long *gala* (bamboo pole). They tried again. Nobody noticed how much time had elapsed. Crowds began to gather on hearing the shouting and screaming. Perhaps someone informed the family. They, too, came there. Along with them came a well-known doctor of that town. He felt helpless for the accidental death. The head of the family said that the person who died had not visited after marriage. He wrote a letter and invited him. This is how it is now, he said, and puffed on several cigarettes, losing his self-control. All the talk, movement, shouts, running around, sorrow, fear, and so on - overall, the incident feels as if it occurred just a minute ago.

Why are you holding my hand? Did I sound too intense? I felt a strong feeling of helplessness. It felt like everyone had become a part of some sorcery. We watched on. A few people came running and panting with a long *gala*. They began to search again. Time was running out. The lady sat over there, holding her crying baby against her chest. Is it sufficient to say that she was washed away by the overwhelming circumstances? Does it suffice to say that she had gone mad in the depths of death? What else can be said? While the men who were searching were fully concentrating on the long poles, the others concentrated on them, too. We stood there and kept standing. Sridhara was critically observing each person there who was related to the dead man. He had surrendered himself to the horror of death. Nobody had the courage to console the woman who was caught in a grave situation.

The river was flowing in front of us as if nothing had taken place. The waves were reflecting the sunlight; on the other bank were the half-submerged, unwavering trees, a reflection of water on the banks at a distance. The lady's distress, people's unending wait, the search for the missing man and so on, and the train sped with a thunderous roar on the railway bridge.

We stood there for hours. The evening was descending slowly. The man with the pole returned to the bank with a pale face. Sridhara looked at him questioningly. He said: "Well, in case the sand shifts and covers it or if it moves forward due to the currents, it would be difficult to find it. Only when the body floats up after three days will it be found". He pointed at the spot where we were sitting and said, "It usually shows up there; it happened so the last few times". Sridhara was marking the entire episode with his eyes. I placed my hand gently on Sridhara's shoulders, and we left.

We have been sitting for the past three days looking at this same view - the same river, sand, boulders, some washermen and fishermen, buses that travel on the bridge, and the train, totally unaware of the days rolling by. Am I right?

In the silence of that night, Sridhara said, "Look, I have come to a conclusion. If, for any reason, you move far away from me, I will jump into the river just like the man you saw today". Sridhara's serious voice sounded funny. I didn't grasp his fears. I thought of teasing him badly. He repeated the same words. I became serious. Once again, the topic of the dead man came up. At that time, when we were surrounded by darkness, fear slowly crept up, and I shivered for a second. Death had surrounded us as well.

Are you saying that it's getting late? In some time, there will be fewer people than now. After they all leave, you and I will wait for Sridhara together. Let us wait until the time we had decided upon earlier.

We came back to the city. The newspapers carried the news of the man who had drowned in the river and that his body was found later. Later, everything returned to normal. Myself and Sridhara, Sridhara and I. I think it would have been so nice if we had remained that way. But what can I do? Is it my fault? I don't have to repent for anything. If you just look at it, Sridhara had undoubtedly made me blossom. By quenching my bodily desires, he had roused me. Just like the physics lecturer used to explain in simple terms, it was like a straight line curve. You, too, know that, don't you?

Having selected Sridhara myself, I had a misconception of exclusivity. The initial few months with him were a mix of somewhat unclear, amiable, painful, and happy intoxication. I had accepted the turn towards such varied attractions. With my interest in cricket and Sridhara's sportsmanship, I had expectations and imagination about Sridhara as a person; slowly, I understood the reality of his character and his temperament. By the time I eventually realised the need to break the barriers and observed the deluge within me, I was introduced to Venkatesha. Did I mention Venkatesha's name? I didn't?

Sridhara was intent on creating his own identity in cricket. He was obviously working hard for his individuality. He was as intensely concerned about me.

Unable to control my curiosity, I once read the short paragraphs he had written about me in his diary and understood his deep love towards me. But what to do – I had slowly begun to move away. My sense of self-love was getting stronger. I began to realise that I had been consumed by passionate love towards Sridhara's game, among other things. From a person who spoke at the speed of electrons, gradually, I became silent. I began to identify myself. The result of this was silence. Silence for hours together; days together of silence. Only then did I experience the true weight of silence. Initially, Sridhara, who was unaware of my background, used to say that I was unwell and force me to meet the doctor. I would try to force myself to laugh and say that there was nothing wrong with me. Later, that, too, became difficult.

Look over there; the pigeons who have made their nests in the arches of the road bridge are returning after their rounds. It is so beautiful to see them fly in flocks. Do you see two boys standing with catapults to hunt the pigeons? Not there on this side. I think those two who are sitting on that side are trying to catch crabs. By the way, the temple up there will be closed soon.

Venkatesha was first introduced to me very casually. He used to visit our home sometimes with Sridhara. Once, as he talked to Sridhara, he just threw a glance at me and finished the coffee that I had served him. I just sat down with a magazine in hand.

He asked me if we could play carrom. So we begin playing the game. I felt a little lighter. I tried not to show that I was not an anxious and restless soul. Once I set my mind to the game, there is no need to try further. Venkatesha kept coming and going. I thought about myself, Sridhara, and Venkatesha. Restlessness and discontent took birth. Venkatesha, who has no great desires, seemed more appealing. Sridhara, on returning from a match, used to say I hit half a century today, or a century today with twinkling eyes. I wouldn't care to listen. Sridhara would look at me with contempt. My love and passion for cricket eventually died. Venkatesha keeps coming and going.

Look, I have a doubt. Perhaps I'm oversimplifying when I narrate to you. Do you feel the same way? Yes? No?

I decided to become single. I protested within. I may feel remorse. I opposed facing a new chapter; I struggled endlessly. I suspected that I had surrendered to Sridhara in a state of innocence and ignorance and wished to avoid getting swept away in the same way again. But Venkatesha's company gave me a wave of excitement, happiness, and satisfaction and showed signs that I might lose my battle of opposition. More than Sridhara or Venkatesha, I had stronger suspicions about my own stance. Once again, I tried to stay single and tested myself. When Venkatesha says let's go out for a stroll, I will refuse. He will go away, feeling bewildered. But one thing was true – I had surely started moving towards him already.

Everything became clearer. I simply waited painfully waited. With suspicion, I waited. Feelings became firm. I saw that it was impossible to tolerate Sridhara any longer. I longed for

Venkatesha. It was impossible to cheat myself. Although I did not hate Sridhara, he became unbearable. That ended my fight against Venkatesha within me. It is beside the point whether I won or lost. I felt it was not possible to live without Venkatesha. I told him. He, too, confided, having gone through a different kind of ordeal. Although Sridhara had suspected it, he didn't believe it when I told him. He laughed. When I repeated with a serious tone, he must have become cognizant of the situation. He sat in front of me, overcome with emotions, and looked at me. There was silence between us. He got up, brought his diary and kept it in front of me. My – our decision was firm. It was dark outside. Time for the dead to rise? He asked me when I would be leaving. I said, tomorrow. Silence once again. He asked me if I remembered our trip to the river. I nodded in fear. If Sridhara appeared to be suffering at times, at other times, I felt like I was suffering. He asked me to reconsider. I told him that I had given it sufficient thought. Then it's fine, he said. Slowly, the darkness was spreading. We sat there for a long time without looking at each other.

Ever since the rift between us had begun, we hadn't slept together. It somehow felt disgusting. That night, not because it was the last time, not because we decided to give in to our intense emotions, not out of pity for each other, not due to a strange responsibility, maybe due to all of these or due to something else altogether, I slept with Sridhara; as an outlet for my-our various compulsions.

I didn't find Sridhara next to me when I woke up in the morning. I searched for him. In the letter on the table, he had written, "You go away with Venkatesha, don't wait for me. You'll never see me again." I tried to grasp its meaning. Immediately, I remembered what Sridhara had said about the river incident. I felt a rush of anxiety. I met Venkatesha and told him that I'd be back after three to four days and came to you. I didn't feel like bringing Venkatesha here. You are well aware of whatever happened thereafter.

We are sitting here, waiting. Look at the reflection of the electrical lights on the water's surface. The evening crowds have dispersed now. I was really scared when a shirt came up with the reeds. The waiting time has ended now. Venkatesha must be waiting. Let us go. Luckily, Sridhara did not drown here and die; that's a big relief.

A Little This Way And That

*R*angaswamy was lying down. He was in a half-awake state. Vehicles were moving about in the road close to his room window. He wished to make his early morning dream come true. He, too, had a role to play in the incident that occurred in his dream. As he remembered snippets of the dream, he wanted to watch how the dream progressed as an audience. He didn't wish to prompt the direction of his dream in any way. Now, he was somewhat successful, and there was a bit of turmoil among the characters in the dream as he watched it. There was also noise from outside. The dream was disturbed. Rangaswamy gave up, smiled and turned.

Just the previous day, Rangaswamy had finished reading a book related to the history of Karnataka. He appreciated the efforts taken by the author. But he was doubtful about some irrational aspects of it. As he pondered about this, he thought it was not possible to state history with certainty.

He could hear the sound of utensils being used. It must have been a while since his wife, Sharadamma, was up. He would have known if the milkman had come. But for the past few days, there was no guarantee that he would come. The previous day, he had to go to a private diary about half a kilometre away to get milk.

Rangaswamy opened his eyes. The room was filled with pleasant light. The ceiling had a few palm-sized wet patches. Each patch was unique. He had worked for three decades in the private sector, looking at numbers. During most of the free time, his eyes were glued to books. Yet, instead of weakening, his eyes had become sharper. He used to observe the wet patches more keenly. Some of them appeared like human faces, like a profile of a woman's face with her hair tied into a knot, a long-faced man, a man with chubby cheeks and a light moustache, a laughing man, a crying man and so on. This was common for Rangaswamy, who was five feet ten inches tall, had a normal build, roundish face and slightly large eyes.

Rangaswamy had another year to retire. He had a desk job at his office. Perhaps due to this, his body was a bit weak. For the past few years, he felt a pull behind his right knee. Even now, when he tried to get up, he felt a pull. He massaged the painful part with his thumb.

Rangaswamy got up. His feet touched the cold floor. There were piles of dusty books on two open wooden shelves, on top of the cupboard, in the attic, and just about anywhere in the room. On the other side, there were a few *panche* (Lungi), shirts, and pants on an old wooden clothes stand. Besides the bed was the table lamp that his friend Lakshmanasa had gifted him twenty years back. The surrounding walls were lacklustre. The door's horizontal beam was broken; the handle was missing a screw and hung down. He thought that he would give a list of all the pending repair work this time to the owner when he came to collect the rent.

He stood near the window. There was an empty side adjacent to his house. On the other side, a house was under construction. They had dug a deep pit in the empty site for the mud they needed for construction. The construction workers walk to work with packed food. In Tamil, they were loudly berating their supervisor, who had cheated on them for their wages the previous week.

Rangaswamy saw Sharadamma's average figure in the kitchen as he walked across the drawing room to the bathroom. Her words followed him. "It's so late, and the milkman hasn't yet come."

He checked the floor before stepping into the bathroom. Every day, at dawn, he woke up to switch on the boiler. He found swarms of cockroaches on the floor when he turned on the light in the bathroom. His throat felt dry for a few seconds as he saw their sheer numbers; he felt as if there had been a relationship between himself and the cockroaches for several decades, and he tread carefully not to squish any of them under his foot. He felt good after washing his face with hot water.

By the time he wiped himself with the towel and came to the hall, Sharadamma brought a milk-filled vessel. Right behind her was their pet Pomeranian dog, Belli.

"Go away, I'll give you later. It wants to be fed before everyone else," said Sharadamma. Although she shooed it away, the dog walked back and sat under the old sofa where Rangaswamy was sitting and stretched itself for a few seconds. Then it got up and started to sniff his *panche*. Rangaswamy lovingly petted the dog.

As soon as he stopped, it came up and stood in front of him. Its body was covered with clumps of white hair with shades of brown. Its marble-sized black eyes calmed down from the petting and love. The face appeared big for the head. Sparse, countable moustache. He stared at all this. As soon as Sharadamma brought the coffee cup, its attention was diverted, and it leapt and ran in a different direction. He smiled and took a cup of coffee.

Rangaswamy had not actively looked to buy the dog. That day, Lakshmanasa had received a cheque for supplying the materials. "Come, Ranganna, let us *quench* our thirst," he said, inviting Rangaswamy. Also, it was a Saturday. It was the day of '*quenching* the thirst' with his friends.

Already, all the people from the office had left. Rangaswamy arranged the files neatly on the table. He took the key bunch, locked the cabinet on top of the table and looked around.

"Now look. We are standing amidst the air that cannot breathe, a dead table and sapless files."

Lakshmanasa was not puzzled. He was used to Rangaswamy's ways over the decades.

"What does that mean, *Guru*? (Friend)"

Rangaswamy looked at Lakshmanasa's light brown complexion and his moving eyes. Then his thick lips moved as if he smiled.

"It's nothing. Come, when *paramatma* (Almighty) enters our stomach now, you'll know. What? Did you think it was as simple as shaving one's head?"

"That's ok. Who else can tease me if it is not for you? Had it been anyone else, I would shave his head off," he said and laughed. Rangaswamy also laughed.

Since morning, once the office opened, the corridor floor was trampled by people walking about; unable to close its eyes and stretch its legs even for a few seconds, it was eagerly waiting for some rest. Noiselessly, he walked on top of it. There, about five feet tall, with a long face, hunchbacked Muneer office attender, saw him with sunken eyes and approached him. It didn't take long for Rangaswamy to guess the reason. It was the same as always.

"What, Muneer, haven't you left for home yet?"

"*Kaiku saab* (Why Sir)? *Jaana hai* (I must go). I just finished with work," he said and looked towards Rangaswamy's pocket.

"No... I won't give you today. Didn't I tell you not to drink every day?"

"*Nai saab, peetha nai, roz peetha nai, pet mein taklif hai* (No sir, I don't drink, I don't drink every day, trouble with my stomach). How can you say this *saab*?"

"Whatever little bit of a collection you've made since morning, isn't it enough? Get lost," said Rangaswamy and gave him a fifty rupee note. He had no doubts as to where his gains of the entire day would be used.

Rangaswamy and Lakshmanasa walked down Kempegowda Road. The road was swarming with so many people that there was no scope even for the shadow to touch the ground. Men and women of all ages- each of them was surrounded by the aura of hurry and anxiety. A din of the vehicles on the road. A variety of items were sold. There, at the base of the tree, which was in the middle of the footpath, sat an old-timer holding up a Pomeranian puppy that looked like a fluffy ball of wool in his palm. He sat still. Rangaswamy stood beside him.

He raised his hand higher and said, "Make my first sale for the day *sahebra*, (Boss) it's a Pomeranian."

Rangaswamy looked. There was another ball of wool near his feet. He wondered why he had started that day's sale so late. He suspected that he might have stolen them. Although he searched all over his eyes and face, there were no such signs.

"What do you say, S*a*?"

"*Mala nako ba* (I don't want). You can take a look if you want."

"*Sahebra*, tell me what you are willing to pay."

"Did you not have any sale today?"

"No... I had some trouble at home, So I came late."

"Did someone give you these puppies?"

Lakshmanasa understood the meaning behind Rangaswamy's words. He simply looked at him.

"Who will give? I have brought them up myself. When we don't have any puppies, I buy and then sell them." Now, there was a smile on Lakshmanasa's lips.

Trying to change the environment that had suddenly turned serious, Rangaswamy said, "So you mean that you sell one or two puppies every day."

"What else can I do? Trouble with my baby girl if I go home. I can't face my wife with empty hands." He was struggling to find words.

Rangaswamy looked straight into his eyes. They seem to tell a lot to him. The person tried in vain to mumble a bit. Rangaswamy spent a few seconds pondering. He wanted to end the conversation. He bought a puppy. He observed the look of relief on the man's face and said, "Let's go. We can't just sit here." He grabbed and pulled Lakshmanasa's shoulder and walked out. Since that day, the Pomeranian dog has become part of his family.

Rangaswamy finished drinking his coffee. As soon as he brought a bowl of milk from the kitchen and said, "Belli, milk!" it came running to its spot. He poured it into its bowl.

Before there were tape recorders in the market, Rangaswamy used to hum songs of *Mukesh, Kalinga Rao, M.S.Subbulakshmi, and Balamuralikrishna* (Singers) in his gruff voice as he got ready to shave. He bought a tape recorder when it was available. Then he didn't have to sing anymore.

More or less, Rangaswamy's day's routine used to begin by leaping into the past. Even now, he was nodding and enjoying *Kalinga Rao*'s songs.

Rangaswamy's father was a well-known Sanskrit Pandit. Due to that, there were many acclaimed books in his house. Over the past three to four decades, Rangaswamy, too, had purchased many books. His father had never asked him to read Sanskrit. Just by observing his father, he gained curiosity in books and then grew fond of reading.

Every Sunday morning, Rangaswamy was used to spending time with children. He used to teach them Sanskrit. It was a game for him, an excuse to watch the faces of children overflowing with happiness. Also, he wished to experience the short-lived, various forms of love, anger, stubbornness, sadness, blame and competition in the children.

2

Rangaswamy left for work. If some faces at the bus stop were familiar, others were unfamiliar. Even though all their faces were lit by the same amount of light, they were not equally happy. They all wore different clothes to suit their profession. The sparkle emanating from their eyes and cheeks was a way to guess their thought processes.

He got on the bus and sat on a window seat. As he looked at the name boards of the shops as if he were new to town, he laughed. The same boards didn't look so new when he walked past them. He wondered why.

It was very difficult to cross the road after alighting from the bus near his office. There wasn't such a crowd even about ten to fifteen years back, he thought. The office lift was out of order. He saw some familiar people, but nobody smiled like they did on earlier occasions. Everyone was hustling about.

Ramaswamy was exhausted after climbing the stairs. He signed in the attendance register before walking up to his chair. As he sat, he massaged the back of his knee. By then, most of my colleagues had come. Just when Rangaswamy had begun to work by spreading open a thick register with numbers written in it,

Puttashamappa said, "Get up, Rangaswamy. Let's have our first dose and come back." "I have just come. Maybe after half an hour," Rangaswamy replied. "I know, addition and subtraction, right? Even if you do it every day and also continue in your dreams, it won't get completed. Come," said the strongly built Puttashamappa. Ramaiah also agreed. When he stepped out of the door, he saw Muneer's sparrow-like body sitting on the stool, his back arched. He smiled at Rangaswamy and took out his bundle of beedis.

As Rangaswamy finished and put the coffee cup down, Venkatesh approached him with a smile. But the smile did not match the crinkle in the eye. "Rangaswamy, I need to talk to you," Venkatesh whispered in his ear. As he looked at Venkatesh, the noise of the coffee cups and the footsteps of the people faded into the distance. "What's the matter?" he asked. Venkatesh walked ahead without responding. Rangaswamy followed him.

Venkatesh was always affectionate towards Rangaswamy; he worked in a bank. He would often visit his good-looking sister with wide eyes, Lalitha, who worked in Rangaswamy's department. He appreciated Rangaswamy for not behaving in an egoistic way. He felt that Rangaswamy interacted with him, although he was two and a half decades younger than Rangaswamy.

In a quiet place, Venkatesh said, "Lalitha has taken leave today. I came to give her a leave note."

"Is that all? There was no hurry for that."

"That's not what I'm here for. It seems yesterday, after returning home from work, she talked to my mother and cried."

Rangaswamy looked puzzled.

"It seems there is some exam in the department."

"What is there to cry for that? She can write and pass."

"Who doesn't know that, Rangaswamy? It seems there is a person in your department who can help you pass the exam."

"Then, that is good."

"No. To help her pass, it seems he forces her to go to movies and hotel rooms with him."

Rangaswamy looked straight at him. This was news to him. He recollected several familiar faces but was unable to guess.

"So?" he asked, deep in thought.

"What do you mean? Tell me if you know. I will take care of him before I leave."

"I have no clue. Will let you know if I find out."

"Lalitha herself could have told, right?"

"She is refusing to divulge out of some fear. Must get it out of her in a day or two."

"Tell her not to be scared. Such people are everywhere. We should just be careful."

Long after Venkatesh left, Rangaswamy felt that he was naïve and lacked experience. His pride in his ability to read all the faces he encounters like an open book is just an illusion. He realised that he could get some idea when he saw people but did not have the ability to dig deep into their psyche. But Puttashamappa and Ramaiah would gather so much news even before dawn breaks. How did they find so much spare time? Slowly, he was convinced that there was a great distance between him and social intelligence.

The air was a bit lighter. He went to his office and looked around at the empty chair, table, cupboard, files, typewriter and other things and felt it had become an island. He laughed softly. After some time, Nanjundeshwara came after a while, and as he saw it, another thought occurred to Rangaswamy.

"I came only to see you, sir."

"Understood. You can take the payment tomorrow."

"Will be happy if that will be done."

"Look, Nanjundeshwar, your head office is in Chennai, isn't it?"

"Yes sir, you must visit us there sometime. You'll have some change. You can relax."

"Let's see then. I need a favour from you."

"Tell me, sir, why not?"

"Someone came from Chennai yesterday. He told me that Jack London's 'People of the Abyss' is available in the Used Book Store near Moor Market. Is it possible to look for it and get it for me?"

"Don't worry. I guarantee you that I'll call and arrange for it today itself," he said and took the details of the book. Nanjundeshwara did not ask what was so special about that book, which records the dreadful life led by the people of East London City, who were in extreme poverty.

Rangaswamy kept himself busy with work until Kapaneepathy came to meet him.

On seeing Kapaneepathi, Rangaswamy was amazed at how his overall figure hadn't changed even a bit over the decades. Only a little hair receded on the forehead, and very few grey hairs peeped out.

Kapaneepathi and Rangaswamy had been classmates until Intermediate. While Rangaswamy buried himself in the books and failed the exams, Kapaneepathi moved around joyfully, completed the exams and obtained the degree. They were staying in a dimly lit, old room. They used to cook themselves. There were enough cockroaches in that small room. They made their homes in the vessels, bookshelves, stoves, toilets and just about everywhere. They would not even allow peaceful sleep for them.

Kapaneepathi worked in the forest department. Over time, he found ways to make money and obtained all that he needed to beef up his body. He would often visit Bangalore and made it a point to meet Rangaswamy every time.

Kapanipathi used to visit Bangalore for an official enquiry against him.

"Pathi, this time, is it a new enquiry or an old one?"

"All wiped out and beheld; there is something special," he said, spreading his palms and waving.

Rangaswamy looked at him in disbelief.

Kapaneepathy smiled and asked, "Don't you read the newspaper?"

"Have you become such a clever cheat that your name is now in the newspaper?"

"Silly! Look here," he said and handed a newspaper clipping to Rangaswamy. Rangaswamy glanced at it. There was news of Kapaneepathi obtaining an award for catching an elephant.

"You caught an elephant? Do you have the *dum* (guts) for it?"

"Am I such a fool? Why would I? Why would I try to catch it and die?"

"Then?"

"I had got a pit dug up for some reason. On its own, the elephant fell into it and got stuck. I called the journalists and told them that I caught it myself," he said and laughed.

"So you mean, you got the elephant for free, and you swallowed all that you got, the size of an elephant?"

Kapaneepathi simply raised his eyebrows. Rangaswamy laughed weakly. He tried to imagine the incident, the way he had behaved at that time, and his celebration. All that seemed like images of a dream.

Rangaswamy mechanically. It was almost five. Lakshmanasa came.

"Why are you looking out of sorts, *guru*?"

"Nothing, just like that."

"What happened?"

"I finished the work that you had written in the letter. The new order for material supply will come by next week."

"Then what else is bothering you?"

"No bother, nothing. Isn't it Friday today, *guru*? Coming. But why is Muneer so quiet, glued to the corner like a mute idiot?"

"Where is he? Haven't seen him all day."

Lakshmanasa began talking about his factory production and about his newly constructed house. Rangaswamy continued to work while listening to all this.

Muneer came, dragging his feet. He looked very frail. Rangaswamy asked him, "What happened to you?"

"It seems this paper belongs to you," said Muneer and gave a letter.

As he took it, Rangaswamy asked, "Did you have lunch?"

"Not anymore. Haven't been able to eat a single morsel for the past three days."

"I warned you not to guzzle. . . Told you that your liver will get gutted. Do you ever listen?"

"That's not it, Rangaswamy. I shouldn't have done that the other day. You see, I spat into the rice that I was eating. That's why…"

Around two years back, Rangaswamy was writing the accounts at the Workers Co-operative Society after office hours. Muneer went there.

"Why did you come here instead of going home straight?"

"If you ask me to leave, I'll go, Sir. I don't have a single paisa (any money) with me."

"Don't lie. You must have already had some and come here."

"Say what you want, but I won't lie."

"Okay, what do you want now?" he asked.

Muneer simply stood there, looking at him.

"I won't give you money. Wait, I'll come."

Muneer sat on a stool with his elbow on his knee and smoked two beedis until Rangaswamy finished his work.

Rangaswamy took him to a bar. Muneer filled some rum in a bottle and lifted it to his lips. Rangaswamy rebuked him and said, "*Bewarsi* (despicable fellow), add some water to it." Muneer laughed and did so.

"If you do this, you'll end up as a roadside corpse."

Muneer kept the glass down. Slowly, he removed some letters from his pocket. He gave one to Ramaswamy. Muneer's address was on it.

"Why are you carrying your own house address?"

"No, Rangaswamy, as you said, what if someday, I fall on the street and die? The corporation people will think the corpse has no family and get rid of it, right? My wife and children must get it, no?" he said and laughed.

"Son of a bitch! Who taught you all this?" said Rangaswamy appreciatively. He had read many books on the impermanency of the body.

They ate *parotta* and *palak paneer* after finishing the rum. Then Rangaswamy asked for the bill.

3

Lakshmanasa came hesitantly to Rangaswamy's house. He wondered what was in store as he knocked on the door and waited for the door to open. There's no problem if Rangaswamy opens the door. But what if it is Sharadamma? Clueless, he looked at the moving vehicles on the road. The door opened. Sharadamma appeared. Lakshmanasa took his eyes off her sullen face with the big *kumkuma* (bindi).

"Is Rangaswamy there?" he asked hesitatingly.

"But what did I tell you when you came so late at night?" said Sharadamma, adding to his turmoil.

"Not like that, but…"

"Then how could you show your face in the morning itself?" asked Sharadamma, just as he had expected. The look she gave him was more intense than her questions. Her eyes pierced through him in disgust as she ignored his question and stepped forward to shut the door.

"Please, just a minute. . ." Her look turned fiercer at his obstinacy. "Nothing, nothing. I came to invite Rangaswamy to

the grihapravesha (housewarming ceremony) of my house."

"Come, come in. He is with the children in the backyard. I'll call him."

"No need. I will go there myself," he said calmly.

Rangaswamy was sitting and teaching the children; his lean chest was bare and visible.

"What is it, Lakshmanasa? You've come so early in the morning. Just another five minutes. It's almost done," he said. Lakshmanasa sat there, leaning against the wall and said, "Didn't I tell you last night itself that I will be coming? You won't remember all that."

The previous day, they had all met for the usual Saturday night drinks. This time, Puttashamappa had joined them. During the first round, they talked about increments in allowance, promotions, and the different ways in which people make almost twice as much of their salary. They sat in a very peaceful place. The nearest table was far enough that they could not overhear any conversations. The surrounding area was dark, with just a dim light over the table.

As he began the second round, Rangaswamy rubbed his nose and took another gulp.

"It's true that we have a stomach along with hands and legs, but above all that, our intelligence is spread all around. . . But look, look, that monstrous Tolstoy writes Anna Karenina even before he turned fifty. Where could be the source of the fire in his belly? He must have so much love for life and about people. Tolstoy is an eminent person.

Puttashamappa was all ears. Rangaswamy ordered another salad. In the dark, Rangaswamy lifted his face up, his eyes cast down and said, "Emile Zola, Pere Cezanne and Van Gogh were friends. Van Gogh is a well-known painter; everybody knows that. But that's not what I want to say. At that time, Van Gogh was mainly into painting landscapes. He got into an argument with his friend over painting women. Zola said that it was important to capture the nerves on the woman's body. Cezanne argued otherwise that it was crucial to paint the entire body. Blood rushed to Van Gogh's eyes. He spent days thinking about it. He was convinced that Cezanne was right. Then he faced a challenge. How to find a nude model? He did not have the means to pay a large sum for that. So, he chose a known prostitute. When she learnt about his strange need, she laughingly told him to cut off his ear and approach. Only then would she agree. She had teased him and sent him away. He did not sleep that night. The next day, he appeared before her. She stood speechless and wide-eyed in disbelief when she saw his extended palm. There was a piece of his ear! If not for that, we probably wouldn't have heard about him. It is just that! The people of his country sing ballads about this. Just look at him, look at those people," said Rangaswamy, and he took another gulp.

This was very typical of Rangaswamy. He used to effortlessly narrate the history of people, culture, politics, and social and literary aspects of different places and regions with gusto.

"Rangaswamy, why don't you take up the all too small departmental exam and finish it off when you have such merit?" asked Puttashamappa without any forethought.

"What is the big deal? Long back, I felt that there was no meaning to all that. What if I get through? I might get an increment of a few hundred rupees. What else?

"How can you say that? That will go on as usual. Even now, it's not too late. Just take the exam for fun. I will take care of everything else." He said that with the intention of increasing Rangaswamy's future in the department. But even before he completed the sentence, Rangaswamy suddenly got up from the chair, held his collar and pulled him with great force. Rangaswamy's leg hit the table, and the bottles on top rolled and fell down. Before Puttashamappa could realise what was happening, he slapped his cheek hard.

"Despicable fellow. Do you invite girls to the hotel on the pretext of helping them pass the exam," he shouted.

Instantly Puttashamappa shrank. Having lost all energy to defend himself and words to reply, he stammered something. He could see Rangaswamy's slightly shaking cheek muscles burning and bulging eyes very close to his face. Rangaswamy, who was losing control, slapped him again. He did not loosen the grip on him. They were pushing each other and moving about. At first, Lakshmanasa didn't know what to do. Then he shouted, "Rangaswamy… Rangaswamy…" and tried to separate the two of them. The people sitting around at other tables got up to see. A few bearers came forward. One of them said softly, "Sir, please don't create a scene here."

"Tell the truth. What did you tell Lalitha? If you are so crazy, you can go and find some awesome ones. Instead, you lustfully go after those who are not interested, *halkat* (Shameless)."

Rangaswamy slowly lifted his head up and sat upright. Lakshmanasa didn't feel like probing any further. They looked at each other. Rangaswamy had still not regained equilibrium. Lakshmanasa placed his hand on his back and said, "Get up…"

When they caught an auto and were on the way, Lakshmana said, "I'll come to your house in the morning. There's some work to do." When they reached Rangaswamy's house, the lamp was still burning in the drawing room. Rangaswamy got down and said, "You can go, Lakshmana." He said, "No, I'll come, wait." He asked the auto driver to wait and walked up with him.

They knocked on the door. Lakshmanasa looked at Rangaswamy's face in the light outside the house. His face and eyes didn't have the animosity as before. Rangaswamy felt guilty for unnecessarily being involved and putting Lakshmanasa in a tight situation. Not knowing what to say, he simply looked at him, placed his hand on Lakshmanasa's shoulders, and smiled at himself.

He went in as soon as the door opened. Lakshmanasa did not hear the door close immediately. He looked back. Sharadamma was standing at the doorstep. Her face was not visible clearly in the dim light. Before he could turn around and leave, she said, "Listen…" Lakshmanasa walked up to her and stood before her.

"I wanted to say something to you." Lakshmanasa did not blink.

"I know that you and him are good friends. Now, I need a favour from you." Lakshmanasa lifted his head a bit questioningly.

"Please don't come home anymore looking for him. You know the reason why."

He heard the burning coal bursting in the cool words, and he was rooted to the spot for a moment. He was aware that Rangaswamy's drinking habit had become worse, and lately, his hands had begun to shake a bit. He sat in the auto, wondering what could be done to mitigate this problem.

During his childhood, Lakshmanasa was very irregular in school. He used to go with his father often to do *kalaai* (inside coating of vessels with tin). Rangaswamy was very close to his father and had spent many nights in Lakshmanasa's house. When he lost his father, Rangaswamy became a kind of wanderer, and Lakshmanasa's father looked after him.

Lakshmanasa remembered the incident that had occurred when he was still doing *kalaai* work more clearly than Rangaswamy. He had done *kalaai* work for about ten-twenty vessels right in front of a rich man's house. His body was burning due to the hot sun, and he was heating up the vessels to do *kalaai* for them. After the work, the hefty woman shifted the vessels back inside. He had packed up his tools and asked the woman for payment. She said, "The owner is not home. Come back later." And had sent him off. Although he was very sweaty, he looked at the big house and returned. Even though he went for three days in a row, he did not even get paid enough to buy a cup of coffee. With a pale face, he had told this to Rangaswamy.

That evening, he raised his voice and spoke in English, and the man softened up. All this was being noticed by his neighbours. The man still did not relent. He yelled, "What is your relationship with him? Go away, I won't pay." "We are partners. We will not move till you pay," said Ramaswamy. He stood there obstinately and had recovered the money.

4

Rangaswamy had been postponing the cleaning and arranging of his room and books. Why not now, he thought. He brought a torn banian from a small pile of discarded clothes. Belli followed him around.

He tied up his *panche* and began to dust and rearrange the books in the same place. He glanced at the unwanted letters and papers that were kept in the books. He threw them away into a pile. The dust made him rub his nose. Belli was sniffing at everything and sneezed due to the dust.

"What work do you have here? Go away," he said, waving his hand as if to hit. As Belli jumped and ran, it banged into the bookshelf and knocked down a few books. Rangaswamy picked them up. He looked at each one of them and put them aside. As he opened the cover and looked into one of them, he saw, 'With Love – Manjula'. He stood still. He read it again and sat slowly on a chair.

He was studying in his second year at that time. By then, he was passionate towards reading. He had bunked the practicals class and sat in the public library. Among the piles and piles of books there, as he walked, looking at the large windows and doors, he used to feel as if he had entered a different world. The floor was carpeted with coir mats to absorb any noise due to movement. Those sitting around reading different books looked like they were in a trance. If he did not finish reading a book in two to three days, he used to feel flat. Even if he pulled Kapaneepathi by his hair, he would not accompany him. "*Lo kudumi* (voracious reader), what is so special? If you want to go to the corporate swimming pool, I'll go with you. We can swim until our body aches," said Kapaneepathi.

Rangaswamy met Manjula in the library. For the first few months, they could only recognise each other. Once, Rangaswamy found a book by Raymond Williams. But he had forgotten to bring his library card. He saw Manjula searching for a book. He mulled a bit and then approached her. "Excuse me," he said. As she turned and looked at him, her gaze didn't seem to cut him off. As a result, he borrowed the book on her card.

Manjula, with a reddish brown complexion, was not a beauty. Ordinary-looking girl. But her energy was enough to shake the earth. But sometimes, she was moody and kept her lips sealed for hours. He became more familiar with all this only after he began to visit her house.

Her father was not rich, only of a middle-class family. He worked at HMT. Yet, he thought that they were better off compared to him. The first time when she invited him to her home, he was very surprised. They talked about movies of Hitchcock, Satyajit Ray, Bimal Roy, and Gurudutt. She said, "My father is a big fan of Gurudutt… Come home and tell him all." He was excited to visit her house again. He washed one pair of pant and shirt out of the two pairs that he owned. At night, he folded it neatly, placed it under his pillow, and wore it to her house the next day. He had not disclosed his latest secret crush to Kapaneepathi.

Rangaswamy was not keen on taking part in the college drama. "I don't have a good voice. I don't want," he said. Yet Kapaneepathi said, "Nobody is asking you to do a musical recital… come on." He had pulled him along. During the drama rehearsal, he didn't have much time for the library, Manjula, her house, or college.

After a great deal of deliberation, he finally invited Manjula to the play. She looked at him and said, "Why are you so shy, like a girl, just to tell me this? I just don't like it." And made him feel at ease.

Although he was sure that she would like to watch the play, he was anxious that she might not. She had come with her father. Just to be sure, he had walked up from the green room to the stage several times and peeped between the two curtains. "Why are you acting as if there's a bear in the audience?" Kapaneepathi had asked angrily.

The next day, as soon as he met Manjula, she clapped and said, "Welcome to the actor."

"Stop joking. How was it?"

"Wait, I'll tell you. Who is that person who took the role of the girl?"

"That is Kapaneepathi. He looked just like a girl, right?"

"Is it enough to just put on make-up and wear the costume? It was awful."

"Then… what about mine?"

"Oh, yours? You didn't even act. You spoke exactly the way you speak here. That's all."

They had both laughed.

Rangaswamy and Manjula had roamed about in crowded places as well as isolated places. He didn't feel anything when they talked. But in a crowd or when they were alone, whenever she looked away, he found her entire body very endearing. Her nose, lips, waist, and full blouse were visible sometimes when the part of her sari moved; all this made his body warm.

Another peculiar thing was when he watched a movie with Manjula, he hid it from Kapaneepathi.

Everything changed after entering the theatre. With only a small source of light for the namesake, the surrounding darkness appeared to have immense power. Manjula's proximity felt very special. The occasional touch of her hand, shoulder and knee made his blood rush. Rangaswamy was unable to pay attention to the screen. After the movie, she was talking about it. But Rangaswamy, who had become one with himself, heard some of it but didn't hear most of what she said.

The headlights of the vehicles were like hitting the targets. In that darkness and light, she carved her figure as she walked home. As Rangaswamy walked back to his room, he couldn't feel the ground beneath his feet.

Manjula was unable to grasp what was going on in Rangaswamy's mind. Rangaswamy, too, was unable to bear his heart to her right away, like the hero in Gurudutt's movie. He also learned the reason why Manjula sometimes withdrew into a shell from her father. He had said, "She's like that Rangaswamy. She thinks she is a very ordinary girl. Not good-looking. Also, love and marriage are not her cup of tea. All that is just bogus, she says." In that case, what about all this activity and mingling? He could not fathom.

Rangaswamy did not know when Manjula and spirituality tied the knot. She would talk about some unknown person and say, "Great soul." He would return, feeling disappointed.

One day, she said, "Do you believe in God?"

"The answer is not as easy as asking the question."

"Why? You trust the driver and travel without worrying when you take the public bus. Can't you do this?"

"That's a different matter. This is different."

"Okay then. Come to the Mythic Society this Sunday. You will learn a lot for yourself. I go there regularly," she said.

"I will do what it strikes me as rational".

Manjula did not turn up to meet him on a few occasions afterwards, although he was expecting.

When they met later, he said, "Look, Manjula. Your way is different than mine. Let us not meet henceforth," he said and left without waiting for her reply.

After this, both their egos had won. They never met again.

He looked at the book again and felt as if he had gone back in time to the love and interaction with Manjula, who had been a part of his life and had just parted ways with her and come back. It was surprising how all this had not vanished. How did the decades disappear in between? Between all this was his domestic life with Sharada, which had all the ups and downs. His Son, his studies, his wedding and all that. Everything had taken place like a movie, all compressed into the frames, rolling by within the timeline. The reversal of time made Rangaswamy laugh. He dusted the book and kept it separately on the table.

"Aren't you done yet? Come for lunch," said Sharadamma as she entered the room.

"It won't be done today. Let it be as it is."

Sharadamma picked up that book, turned the pages and looked up.

"Who is this Manjula?"

Rangaswamy looked at her. Peaceful face. Pure curiosity in her eyes.

"I used to go around with her during college. I probably could have married her, too. But I didn't even try," he said, laughing softly without any hesitation.

"Did you love her a lot?" she asked a question like a gentle ray of light.

"Ah… yes… a lot."

Rangaswamy did not stutter. He just did not feel at ease talking about love, that's all. He was following Sharadamma's eye movements. They looked the same, soft and gentle. The smile on the corner of her mouth was devoid of any sarcasm or malice.

She placed the book gently on the table and said, "Get up. It's time for lunch."

"Did you give lunch to Belli?" he asked as he followed her.

He felt disoriented as soon as he woke up from the afternoon nap. He had had a disturbed sleep. Broken and disjointed dreams. Rows and rows of faces. Many faces were patched up with parts of Manjula's face.

He got up and washed his face, drank coffee and continued to arrange the books. He finished it by sunset. Rangaswamy was tired. He asked for another cup of coffee and drank it. Sharadamma handed him the list of items to be purchased in the market along with an empty bag.

Rangaswamy turned around and looked as he stepped into the street. Belli had thrust its nose between the rods of the gate and looking at him. He walked ahead.

Some children were already bursting with crackers outside their houses. The small lamps lit on the compound walls and flat terraces of the houses on either side of the road were spreading tenderness. In some other houses, children were walking with excitement around the compound. Green, red and yellow lanterns were gently swaying in the portico of some other houses.

The market was buzzing with activity. There were streams of colourful lights at all the shop entrances. On seeing the lights streaming all along the road, the light on the electric pole in the street was looking for a way to hide itself. Throngs of people were walking and standing anywhere and everywhere.

Swamy bought something in a shop and looked around. He saw a couple with a daughter. They were going to enter the next shop but changed their mind and came to the same shop where Rangaswamy was present. On seeing the woman, Rangaswamy got a doubt. The man was asking for something from the shopkeeper. Only half the face of the woman was exposed to light. Rangaswamy was a bit hesitant. He saw clearly only when she turned towards him. Rangaswamy looked at her keenly. Unable to restrain himself any longer, he went up to her.

"Excuse me. . . Aren't you Manjula?" he asked in a low tone.

She looked at him as if he was a stranger. "Yes... And you?"

"Rangaswamy. . . Do you remember?" He asked, looking at her face.

"Oh yes! . . It has been several years." Memories were glittering in her eyes.

"Who is this, *amma*(mother)?" her daughter whispered.

"This is Rangaswamy, an old acquaintance."

Rangaswamy looked at her as she looked at him with great curiosity.

"This is my daughter, Madhuri. We are visiting her."

"What is your son-in-law doing?"

"He is an engineer in a TATA company."

By then, her husband had joined them.

"This is Rangaswamy . . . My husband," she said, looking at them. They both greeted each other.

"*Amma*'s old acquaintance," their daughter explained.

"Very nice. You continue. I'll be back," he said and went off to another shop. Madhuri followed him, saying, "I'll come too."

Now, Rangaswamy saw Manjula in a new light. There was absolutely no hesitation in her. There was only a childlike friendliness. He compared her present self to Manjula, whom he knew decades back. She looked very much run-down.

"I'm fine. . . And you?" He asked, looking at the dark patches around her eyes.

"I'm fine," she replied, avoiding eye contact with him. Rangaswamy felt uncomfortable.

"Is your wife in good health? How many children?" She asked, looking at his sagging shoulders.

"Just one son. He lives in another city with my daughter-in-law."

"So, no more responsibilities," she said, laughing.

"Same with you, right?"

"How come? Especially my other daughter . ." She was about to say something when the man and his daughter came back.

"Shall we leave now?"

"Her house is close by. Do visit when you have the time," she said and looked at Madhuri. She wrote down her address and gave it to him.

After they left, Rangaswamy went to a few other shops. On his way home, he thought he must tell Sharada about meeting with Manjula. He remembered the manner in which Manjula had stopped in the middle while telling about her other daughter. He wanted to know all about it. He thought that he had the address anyway. He searched his pocket. He didn't find the piece of paper Madhuri had given.

He stood still for a moment and then moved on.

The Shift

That day was also just like any other day. Nothing special. With a greater precision than the wall clock, the inner clock woke him up at six o'clock sharp. An amusing dream just a second ago. Standing in line to race with tens of people at the sound of the whistle, running as if his entire life depended on it, came to an abrupt end as Rangaswamy opened his eyes. Wearing a white T-shirt and blue shorts, his blood pressure rising, and a row of sweat beads around his neck, he ran. As his feet touched the ground, his mind was way over the top. But that gusto stopped there. Somehow, he found a relationship between his dream and his mind and laughed. Later, with waves of balance, he saw a joyful and playful dance in the light streaming through the window. As a mark of gratitude to it for fully waking him up, Rangaswamy shook his body and hands and got up more energetically. The rest of the morning chores went as per the clock. The slightly dark-skinned, five and-three-quarters feet tall, past middle-aged man's waist size was a bit much. For the past few years, his doctor had been asking him to try to reduce it by two inches. Five years back, if his wife Vimalamma had not died suddenly due to a brain haemorrhage, maybe she would have forcibly made some difference to his waist size. Maybe her wish would have been fulfilled, at least a little bit.

Whatever it is, her wish to get her son Vishwanath married was fulfilled. When she began to insist on him to get married, just like youngsters these days, he said, 'What is marriage?' and 'Is that even required?'. Some time passed since he had uttered such words and walked away. When they got Ragini's proposal, they brought it up to him in a careless manner with the thought, 'How will he agree, don't we know?'. But they were all surprised to see his disinterest turn into interest. More than her work and other things, more than her curly hair and facial features, it was not clear if it was probably Bendre's poem, '*Modalagiththi...*' rendered by her melodious voice or the beautiful handwriting in her letters that looked like a pigeon's footsteps. Everything happened suddenly, within just a week's time. Both the parties were in a state of urgency. Vishwanath's family felt as if they were riding a mechanical horse. Ragini's family felt as if they were flying in the *Pushpaka Vimana* (mythical flying chariot).

Rangaswamy felt that his wife Vimalamma's eyebrows were truly topped with the Holi festival for some days due to Vishwanath's wedding. Then what about his daughter Surabhi? Words fell short for that. What could be said? He wondered what more could be said when her words, behaviour and expressions were uncontrollably overflowing. Due to this, he began to feel that life was very simple and beautiful and had quietly stood with his eyes wide open in amazement.

Just when he began to feel secure, he was hit by Vimalamma's brain haemorrhage like a slab of stone. It is pleasant to fill up with beautiful and happy things and sail together. But such an unexpected beating? He remembered that day as if he was in a daze. Even later, during the silence between some other conversations, unknowingly, that memory would creep in and weigh down on his eyelashes. There, he could only see a few images. Vimala's body was laid down in the hall. Relatives who sat in and out of the house, wherever they found some space. The soft-footed air was flowing among them, and so were their weird postures. Snippets of their whispered talks and the priest who did the funeral rites and later the crematorium. Especially that – all this grew as big they could and broke the words that came to mind. Then it would be difficult for him to get things back in order and continue.

Often the surrounding noise would just stop and he would suddenly feel lonely in the middle of several people. Then the more he clenched his fist to stop it, the graph of worries only rose higher. Out of these, one main point caught his attention. In all aspects, he could more or less intuitively predict and tell precisely, categorically and harshly, many things about all their relatives. But then how did it fail regarding his own wife? He could not understand how it slipped away like sand from a fist. At such moments, not only other people, he couldn't even trust his own self. There was no way out as that feeling intensified and took the form of a deep sigh. Even that day was a repeat of the same thing.

The same beats on that day too, just like any other day. As soon as he stepped out for a walk, the early morning sunlight and the light breeze gently patted his back, increasing his walking speed. The faces that were usually seen in the park exchanged smiles. Words that everyone knew, and anyone could say were moving about in the folds of the breeze there. He, too, pulled out a few from there and shared it with the people around him. By the time he got back home, his son and daughter-in-law would have finished the morning chores at bullet train speed, and the afternoon lunchbox would also have been ready.

Once they left, the house felt much bigger than it was. It was as if the air could easily breathe and gave the opportunity to move about freely in the hall and rooms. Earlier, he, too, used to ride the scooter. But once he hurt his leg badly, and the doctor gave him a prescription permitting him to only drive a car, he followed that even if it pinched his pocket a bit.

Rangaswamy was used to doing all his work methodically and without feeling bored. He did not want anyone else's help. He believed that this kept himself and others happy. Vishwanath-Ragini never expected or wanted his help in any of the daily routines. Sometimes he would take the initiative and put clothes in the washing machine, tighten the screw of the cooker lid and do other small things around the house.

Although he did not hold a very high post in a private company, he held a mid-level job. He had his own chamber. There was a certain pleasantness in the way the table, chair, fan, cupboard, tray with files and other things were arranged there. The tiles on the floor of the corridors inside the office appeared alert due to the movement of familiar people and welcomed everyone in hushed tones. Apart from this, some people were busy trying hard to wake up the lazy handrail, wash basin and other things in the vicinity. As if in continuation of this, mild light slowly stepped in. The cool breeze was blowing here and there in support.

As Rangaswamy sat in his chair and began his usual work, everything went back to normal – even the office attender Narasimha's salute. As usual, Rangaswamy picked up the file from the tray on the left side of the table and began his work. Then, one thing followed the other. Drafts, notes and also telephonic conversations. Attendees would bring in files, keep them, and take files away. A few people would come and go for office work. Only when Narasimha served him coffee did he realise that it was past twelve o'clock. The coffee tasted even better when his colleague Muniyappa entered with a cup in his hand at that moment. As soon as he saw him, Rangaswamy said, "Ah, look, the answer to your riddle just flashed to me today." "Very good. So, tell me what it is then," he replied and looked at Rangaswamy. The strange behaviour began right then. His hand seemed to hang and fall, and the coffee cup fell, as Muniyappa kept calling, "Rangaswamy... Rangaswamy..." his face leaned to a side. And his right leg, too. Muniyappa immediately recovered from the shock, and as he shouted, "Narayana... Narasimha... Venugopal... come fast..." they all came running, along with a few others. If some of them held Rangaswamy's hand, others tried to move his leg to the side. Srikantha, who witnessed this episode, realised that Rangaswamy had a stroke.

Immediately, if the blood pressure of the office people went up a bit, all the things there were slightly dazed, as if they were impacted by a blow. The air felt under pressure. Those who were around Rangaswamy's chamber, "Why... How... Healthy person..." and other words were floating around. Nobody was clear whether he was conscious or not. They were looking at Rangaswamy's shivering hand and leg. Amidst all this, Srikantha said, "Let's not wait for his son... Let's just inform him... quick, quick... shift... we will not waste time," and called the ambulance from a nearby hospital and shifted him. Soon, Vishwanath, who had heard the news, joined them. He was told that by then, Rangaswamy had been sedated by the nursing home. He sat there looking at the remaining blood tests, BP, ECG, and other treatments that were being given systematically. He came to terms with the seriousness of the situation and did not forget what had to be done immediately. Ragini, who was working on the outskirts of the city, said she would come, sounding worried and curious.

By evening, the situation became a little clearer. Rangaswamy was very perturbed by the happenings. As the doctor examined him in many ways in order to diagnose him, he felt like an onlooker, but he tried to keep his curious and anxious mind under control and listen. He tried to grasp any signs, as much as he could, from their talks. The doctor told Vishwanath that although there was no danger to life, Rangaswamy had a stroke on the right side. Although there was no way to determine the cause, he went ahead and prescribed medicines and told him about the daily physiotherapy and other things that were required to improve his constitution. He also explained his condition to Rangaswamy, and finally smiled and said, "Don't worry," and gently placed his hand on his shoulder.

Shocked at the sudden turn of events, Rangaswamy felt as if he had turned into a different person altogether. He tried to feel his shaking right hand with his left hand. But he couldn't feel the touch. Although he had guessed that this might happen, only then did he realise the extent of it. He tried to move his hand some more; he couldn't. At that moment, everything seemed to stand still; he took a deep breath and swallowed. Then he opened his eyes, and after a few seconds, he slowly stroked his right knee with his left hand, although he found it a little difficult. No, he could not feel anything. He stroked his right cheek. It was the same, no different. He just turned his face and looked on as if he was seeing and not seeing something. At that time, he was completely oblivious to anyone who was walking around his bed. Somewhere, some bright light and elsewhere, some dull light appeared. Along with that were the wandering whispers. Among all this, he spent the rest of the time awake, filled with thoughts on what might have caused this change in his condition. The use of this was a big zero and ended up giving him a headache.

People from Vishwanath's, Ragini's and his office visited Rangaswamy in small groups. "Just obligation," Vishwanath told Ragini, for which she posed a question, "Friends and relatives?" and said, "That, too, is the same." Vishwanath smiled as if in appreciation of her analysis. Later, as he sat watching the single riders on two-wheelers and cars going by on the road, he suddenly gave her a stare as if he had a sudden thought: "Shall I ask?" For that, she shook her head as if to ask, "What?" He stared right into her eyes and whispered, "How about us…?" Perhaps she was going to say something. Just then, "How is he…" said the doctor as he walked in and released the tension. Ragani was somewhat relieved for not having to reply. Rangaswamy did not feel like finding out what people around him would say in low tones to Vishwanath and Ragini; he just gazed at the light that peered in through the gap in the curtains and the images that it created on the wall.

After bringing Rangaswamy home, they had to alter the timings of all the work to suit the situation. He could not be independent in any way. Rangaswamy thought that he was not very different from the sofa, TV, teapoy and other things in the house. This feeling sometimes pushed him into thinking that he had become very weak. As a result, Rangaswamy, who had never asked for anyone's help for his personal needs, was forced to do so. He was agonised that those days were gone and it would just remain a memory. The present reality had not just shaken him mildly. The deep-rooted desire that somehow the condition of his body might attain enough strength to support his mind and thoughts had become one with his pulse. Even in this extreme situation, he wondered how he was able to sleep almost as well as before and asked the doctor about it. He said, "That is a gift to you by the almighty," making him smile.

As usual, as soon as Rangaswamy opened his eyes at six in the morning, Vishwanth-Ragini distributed the work between themselves. The wheelchair was essential for his movement. They had to help him get out of bed, brush his teeth, take him to the toilet, and do other things. Rangaswamy only had to cooperate as they tried to help him. Nobody realised the six and seven days that passed by with these kinds of adjustments. Rangaswamy could feel that his right hand and leg, which were affected by the stroke, were shaking more and more. It was also established that they had absolutely no sensation. As per the doctor's advice, Vishwanath had to take Rangaswamy to the hospital for physiotherapy. But that did not sustain for long. There was a need to arrange for private physiotherapy. But then they began to realise that solving that issue was not very easy. The issue looked as big as a mountain. They usually got the same response everywhere they enquired: that it was not possible to bring all the necessary physiotherapy instruments home. But one day, they got the solution from the same doctor who was treating him. This happened only because of the respect that the physiotherapist Shekhara had for the doctor.

Shekhara had a squarish face, was tanned, was about thirty years old, and had a strong body and sharp eyes. Since the doctor had already informed them about his fees and the things required for his treatment, there was very little talk about everything when he came with a bag. Other than just observing one another and drinking the coffee that Ragini brought, there was nothing much else.

Vishwanath asked, "When will you start?" for which, "What do you mean when... today itself..." said Shekhara. Vishwanath was happy that he didn't have to take Rangaswamy to the hospital from that day itself. Immediately, Rangaswamy gave a more thorough look at Shekhara. After he gently explained the procedure he was going to follow to Rangaswamy, he began to pay attention to the first day's treatment and tried to follow the instructions completely. He liked Shekhara's words, behaviour, the structured way of working and so on. The physiotherapy issue was resolved, and the issue of how Shekhara would make his visits when both of them would leave for work was not such a big problem for Vishwanath. Since people who lived three houses away agreed to give and collect the key, it was very convenient.

The next day onwards, Shekhara came exactly at the scheduled time. He brought with him a fist full of new light and a hand full of new air. He spoke less. The work he did was supported by his pure heart. With every passing day, they became close, and a little bit of affection grew. Shekhara did his work with ease, with minimum instructions and talk in between, and a glimpse of a smile here and there.

There were no difficulties in Shekhara's work. Even if there were, they were very minor. And that too only from Rangaswamy's side. He found some happiness and sometimes a feeling of joy for having found a person without any expectations; not only did he do the physiotherapy, but he also behaved in a pleasing manner. He thought that although it was true that he was moving in an endless circle, the few instances that erased some of his loneliness made him feel lively. As a response to his talks, Rangaswamy began to say some incomplete words, which brought happiness not only to him but also to Shekhara. It was in those moments that he was surprised that even on his half lips, lines of laughter were possible. When he realised that it was real, he gave Shekhara a look of gratitude.

Some days, Shekhara used to cut the calls on his mobile. Rangaswamy guessed that they were unwanted calls. Later, when he did the same in the next few days, he motioned Shekhara to take the call. After his conversation, Shekhara seemed to be in some turmoil. Without any way of finding out about it, Rangaswamy remained quiet.

That day, when Shekhara was working, he got a call, and then Rangaswamy felt that he appeared to be in some kind of a dilemma. Rangaswamy gave him a questioning look as he was taking much longer to finish his work. He said, "It's not important… my mother has to be taken twice a week for dialysis… sometimes he skips," he said. Rangaswamy lifted his head up. "The same… my uncle's son… He takes good care, but sometimes he doesn't come in time. I must find someone else, but until then…" and bent his neck down as he worked. However, Rangaswamy appreciated Shekhara's mental grit and felt that things could take on any level. He motioned him to stop his work and said, "Now you go… my work can wait…" and touched his shoulder and told him slowly so that he could understand. He nodded slightly and left in the hot sun. Later, Rangaswamy wished that only someone could create an instrument to measure all kinds of agony, and he just let out a sigh.

He returned in the afternoon. Rangaswamy felt that his face appeared relaxed. Shekhara finished his work without allowing him to talk. Only later, Rangaswamy gestured with his left hand as if asking him to explain everything in detail. Shekhara explained everything in just a few words.

"Ours is an ordinary middle-class family. *Appa* (father) had a government job. There's a five-acre property in the native place. Even that hit the ground in my cousins' deceit. *Appa* was a cigarette and gambling addict. If not for *Amma*'s smartness, we would have rolled down the ditch long back. *Appa* would just roam around. When *Amma* got my sister married, it was an uphill task. My brother-in-law has his own business in a far-off place. Average income. In all this chaos, nobody bothered about me, who secretly yearned to become a doctor. Finally, the damned cigarette did not spare *Appa* and took him as a sacrifice. Just when we thought that a big chapter was closed, another one emerged. That is *Amma*'s sugar complaint. Although she had diabetes for a long time, we had not paid attention to it. Only after it shot up did we realise. It did not come down, no matter what. Even though the kidney failed and has reached the dialysis stage, I forgot to mention one more thing. Even before all this, my maternal uncle's son was staying with us and pursuing his studies. For some reason, *Amma* is extremely fond of him. And he feels the same way about her. Now he has finished his studies and joined a good job. But he has his eyes set on money. He has a great opportunity for that in his current job. Let it be. It's not that he himself had insisted on taking Amma for dialysis. Sometimes, he acts as if he has gone crazy, but he can't say when. That is the only problem. Let it be about myself, that person who treated you helped me learn all this -" he said. After he had finished, they both sat quietly for some time. Rangaswamy allowed all that he heard to go down and spread itself. The sun was setting outside.

As the months rolled by, Rangaswamy began to feel a bit confident about himself. He was a little excited about the breeze and felt enthusiastic to play in the moving shadows. In the presence of Shekhara, he began to try walking a little bit with the help of his walking stick. It was during this time that he began to feel somewhat lonely at home. He just kept thinking. The one who used to talk so much in the office, go out of his way and talk to everyone, lighten the load of work and make the time fly was all alone like this. He was unable to open up at home like he did at work. Perhaps because somebody or someone else continued to visit him at least once a week, they would reminisce about the past and laugh. If they saw him even make an effort to laugh in response, they would laugh louder. Sometimes, Vishwanath-Ragini found this peculiar, and they, too, joined in the laughter. That was rare. After Vimalamma's death, the rift between the family members and the extent of it was well known anyway. Now, all the more so. Now, unable to move his limbs properly, he was like a child, and the somewhat full and somewhat empty Shekhara was like a child in some other way, he thought. Rangaswamy could fully open up his mind and layers of emotions without any hesitation, and even in this plight, he could laugh wholeheartedly, sometimes even cry, and all this made him happy. This happened due to Shekhara's way of talking. His way of completely analysing the unwritten strange incidents of the family and relatives, stories in the books that opened his eyes, scenes in the movies that he watched, and truly the crazy dances in every field was the reason behind it. Due to this, Rangaswamy felt waves of happiness when Shekhara came. Sometimes, he thought it was good that he suffered from the stroke. He even got some strange thoughts that he would be able to see a few such warm days.

People from Rangaswamy's office continued to visit him. But he knew that he couldn't get back to office. He was physically incapable. Hence, unemployed. Not only that, he had zero income. In every way, he was dependent. Who did he depend upon? Vishwanath-Ragini, right, such thoughts swirled around often. Helpless, he quietly looked at the shadows spreading outside the window.

That evening, he had some crazy enthusiasm. As he sat looking out of the window, watching the stars, he picked up his walking stick, and with some hesitation, he tried to get up and walk slowly. Immediately, he smiled. He was able to walk. Without thinking, he walked towards the hall. Vishwanath and Ragini were talking after dinner. He tried to get back. But he thought he heard something and stopped. Immediately, he realised. They were talking about him. He held on tight to his walking stick.

"How many more days do we have to take care of him?"

"What do you mean by how many days?... This is a terminal case, you understood, right?"

"That means, as long as he's alive... scary to think about it."

"It's difficult to find a caretaker for him... also an additional burden."

"Now that he's going to lose his job, there will be no contribution from him... zero."

"So now only a burden... like a rock on our heads."

"One hundred percent a burden."

"Then our future... completely destroyed, right..."

"Not just that... also our freedom..."

"That means our plans to renovate the outhouse and improve has failed, right?"

"As of now, no escape..."

"No escape, that's it..."

As their words repeatedly hit him, he took the support of the wall along with his walking stick and with great difficulty, he reached his room, drank a glass of water and lay down on the bed, stretching out his body; he closed his eyes. Unlike drinking water, the words 'burden', 'future is completely destroyed', 'no freedom', 'terminal' and others were very difficult to take in. They surrounded him, heated up his body and a thin layer of sweat could be seen around his neck and all over his forehead.

He slowly began to realise the weight of the silence of the outer world. It would be different if he had the desire to be alone, but what if he felt lonely due to strange circumstances? When he saw that all that he had thought and wanted together tumbled and rolled away, everything was just empty. It was a kingdom of only zeros, he felt. He could tolerate everything else, but 'burden', 'a rock on our heads' were unbearable. After some time passed, he thought that there was no use in preaching to them; they had their own ways.

In the morning, as usual, all the chores happened wordlessly. Vishwanath-Ragini left after completing all the work. Later, Rangaswamy went up to the cupboard and opened the door with difficulty and picked up his degree certificate, which he had kept with a lot of pride, all the certificates of achievement from his office, and some things that he was mad about and kept close to his heart; he took them all and threw them in the corner of the compound. He stood there staring at them for a few seconds. Later, he struck the match stick, lit it on fire, and stood staring at it until they were all burnt to ashes. The whole time, only he himself and the fire before him existed, and the rest were all zero. Later, he raised his head. Just like the scene changes in the blink of an eye in the movies, he felt that the familiar house, things and people had changed in an instant and smiled. Only then did he feel the heat of the sunlight hitting his face, and he walked inside.

That evening, when Vishwanath-Ragini was walking about the house, they looked like keyed-up dolls. He felt like this was nothing special. Not knowing what to do, he peered into the darkness and closed his eyes quietly.

The next day, although Shekhara was performing his duties as usual, Rangaswamy began to feel as if he was looking at him much more than usual. That day, he said, "Are you unwell… somehow you are looking different…" for which he laughed and said, "Nothing of that sort," and waved his hand. Later, he changed the topic and enquired about his mother. "It's going on. I can read the newspaper if you want…" he said and cheered him up.

Shekhara's visits for Rangaswamy's treatment continued without any hitch. Within a few months, he became familiar with the due dates for their current bill, water bill, phone bill and the online mode of paying them. Also, he learnt about the days when they would get water supply, the necessary plumbing and carpentry work for the house, the grocery shop and the shopkeeper, his name and the distance from the house by talking to them. "Isn't it the day that we get water supply, madam…?" he would ask Ragini as if to remind her to store the pure tap water for drinking and cooking purposes. As he said that, Rangaswamy would look at him, and his shoulders would jump slightly.

More than all this, Vishwanath hated giving the grocery list to the shopkeeper but was compelled to do so. Once, unable to bear the look of his grumpy face, Shekhara said, "Well… just one thing… I'm almost done with today's work. I can give the list on my way back. I know which store and all that." Vishwanath was so happy to hear that. "That's okay…" he said, but handed over the grocery list to Shekhara. Once he lightened his load and left, Rangaswamy waved his palm as if to ask, "Why did you do this?" Shekhara just replied with a smile. But this didn't stop there. During the time he spent in their house, not only did he have to receive the groceries that were delivered, but he also checked whether it was all in order, and if something was amiss, he had to take the necessary steps. Due to this, Shekhara became very familiar with everything related to that shop, and since he became a part of the household work, Vishwanath-Ragini has been very happy. They were rid of the pressure of getting back home at a particular time and also the need to finish all the housework themselves. As a result, whenever they spoke to Shekhara, strands of trust began to fly and reach him. And Shekhara began to reciprocate with pleasing behaviour rather than with words. Without being told by anyone, he dedicated himself to taking care of Rangaswamy. More than the energy that was slowly being replenished by physiotherapy, the lines of worry that were emerging on his forehead decreased.

That day, Shekhara was expected in some time. Thinking that he would surprise him by preparing some coffee, holding on to his walking stick, he got up and turned on the tap in the kitchen to wash the vessel to prepare coffee. He fell, and the walking stick rolled too far for him to reach. He haggled a bit and moved his hands, trying to get up. It was just not possible. In all this, the tap water kept running. He tried a few more times in vain. The sink began to overflow, and... he wondered if he could shout and call someone for help. But there was nobody next door at that time. And the people who were given the keys to his house lived a bit far away. How do we inform them? Vishwanath-Ragini? He couldn't think beyond this. He just turned, scooted, and sat with his legs stretched out, leaning against the wall. The water kept flowing. For some time, he watched the direction in which it was flowing, the rising levels and other things. His heel was soaked. He just sat quietly. The water level kept rising.

After some time, the front door opened. Shekhara was startled to see the water that had almost reached the front door and rushed inside. Rangaswamy stared at him unblinkingly. The first thing he did was to turn off the tap. He immediately went to the hall and got a chair. Then he ran to the front door. He called out to a few people for help. Some people who were aware of his visits came to help. Giving directions and all of them talking together, they made Rangaswamy sit on the chair. Rangaswamy looked at them, moved his lips and nodded. Those who had come did not just stop at that, but they also helped to gather all the water that was spread out on the floor and filled up the bucket to throw it all out. Once the situation was brought under control, Shekhara said, "Thanks", for which they just pointed at Rangaswamy and said, "Please take care of him," and left. Later, Shekhara found a dry piece of cloth and wiped the floor. Then, as if nothing had happened and everything was as usual, he finished his work and said, "Just have your lunch and sleep," and left without giving way for Rangaswamy to speak.

Evening, after Vishwanath-Ragini returned home, three-four men and women came. Without talking much, they described that day's event, and in a preaching tone, they told them to ensure that it doesn't happen again. Vishwanath-Ragini felt uncomfortable. They were also angry at Rangaswamy for not telling them until then. Vishwanath said, "If you had just called me once, I would have arranged everything... look what happened now... what not..." Ragini also said some words in his earshot and some away. Rangaswamy did not reply to anything and kept quiet.

One day, Vishwanath spread out a drawing in front of Rangaswamy. "We can get good rent if we renovate the outhouse a bit… True, it involves a bit of expense. She and I will take care of it…" he said. Rangaswamy said, "No need of yours… I will get it, and then we will see." He mixed clear and unclear words and closed the topic. Puzzled, they looked at each other.

In the next three or four days, Shekhara avoided any face-to-face conversations with Rangaswamy. The following day, he did not even show up. Rangaswamy waited for him. He was bound by worries along with tiredness. The day passed by. And the next day, too. Only the hours passed without any use. He got up. He wore his dress however he could, locked the house, got down to the street and caught an autorickshaw.

Evening, when Vishwanath and Ragini returned home, they were very surprised. Also perplexed. A feeling of some impending doom and some doubts along with it. On enquiring with the neighbours, they were no less surprised by what they heard. They were terribly confused. They didn't know whom to call. Rangaswamy's was switched off. What about his friends? They didn't know. They also contemplated lodging a police complaint. Later, Vishwanath suddenly got up as if he had an idea. Even as Rohini asked, "What are you doing…" he opened the drawer of the table to see if he could find any piece of paper or something. When he didn't find anything, they just sat quietly for a little while longer. Later, they got up, walked out and sat on either side of the door. There was half-light ahead of them. Half opened door behind them. The gate in front of them shook sometimes as if posing a question to them. A few aimless thoughts were flowing here and there. If it was enough to fill Vishwanath's head, it was a fistful for Ragini. Sometimes, cars, bike scooters, and other vehicles spread some light as they passed by, and they made different sounds. Along with them a few familiar and forgotten words. Many types of arrangements were unable to take shape. Clueless, they just sat waiting.

Later, after some time elapsed, a cab stopped in front of the house. Vishwanath-Ragini stood up. Shekhara got off and carefully helped Rangaswamy off the cab. Vishwanath-Ragini felt some weight being lifted off their bodies. They also felt that the situation was under control. The surrounding air eased up, and they felt like stepping towards the cab, yet they didn't. Within a few seconds, Shekhara's mother, along with his uncle's son, also got off. Vishwanath-Ragini looked at each other in surprise. Rangaswamy walked up a few steps with a small smile and stood aside, pointing with his finger. All of them walked towards the outhouse with their belongings. As he walked past Vishwanath-Ragini with a smile, they did not react. They looked at him quietly. And they kept looking.

www.ingramcontent.com/pod-product-compliance
Lightning Source LLC
LaVergne TN
LVHW041703070526
838199LV00045B/1183